QUIET HOUSES

SIMON KURT UNSWORTH

The stories in 'Quiet Houses' represent a big leap forward in terms of quality for talented newcomer Simon Kurt Unsworth, and this marks the book out as easily his best and most cohesive work to date. Taken as a whole, the collection is quietly impressive, quietly ambitious, and loudly terrifying. The tales, as well as the uneasy atmosphere and the common themes running throughout, are all held together by a cunning conceit, and it is this linking story that makes the whole far greater than the sum of its parts. - *Gary McMahon - Pretty Little Dead Things, Pieces of Midnight*

A major new talent in the horror genre...essential reading for lovers of weird fiction. - *Pete Tennant, Black Static Magazine*

A compelling and sensitive portrayal of the power of place, and the resonance of memory - *Tom Fletcher - The Leaping, The Thing on the Shore*

Here's a writer who irritably scratches at the uncanny in the everyday, but whose skill is admirably suffused by a thorough grounding in the art of past masters of the macabre. These stories set out to fill the reader with dread - and do - but what they leave you with, and what makes them special, is a churning of the emotions bordering on tenderness. Bottom line: they don't let you go. Terrific stuff from a rising star. - *Stephen Volk - BAFTA Award Winning Author of Ghost Watch, Afterlife*

With Quiet House, Simon Kurt Unsworth further establishes himself as a major voice in fantasy and horror. Within its pages, the reader will find wonderfully chilling ghost stories linked by a wraparound device that makes the book more than a collection of tales. That's as it should be, for like all of Unsworth's work, *Quiet House* defies categorization. No summary can do it justice. The book must be read, savored, contemplated, and read again – preferably in a quiet room where something not-quite-seen watched from the shadows. - *Lawrence C. Connolly, VOICES*

[Lost Places is] an excellent debut...One of the best of the year. - *Ellen Datlow*

All those of you who bought Simon Kurt Unsworth's first collection – hang on, can we have a show of hands here? What? You DIDN'T buy it? Go and rectify this error immediately! – all those of you who DID buy it, as I was saying, will know that his excellent short stories range across a wide swath of that territory we like to call The Weird. The Weird can be found in all the old familiar regions of supernatural fiction, the shunned house, the spooky woods; however, and maybe more interestingly, we can also come across it in bright new places – places as unlikely as a holiday swimming pool, or as exotic as a mining site in Africa. Simon's talent is such that he brings The Weird with him wherever he goes, and this holds very much true in this, his latest collection. Which, of course, you also need to buy. - Steve Duffy, International Horror Guild award-winning author of *The Rag-And-Bone Men*

This book is a work of fiction. Names, characters, places, events, and incidents either are the product of the author's imagination or are used fictitiously. Any resemblance to actual persons, living or dead, or locales is entirely coincidental.

www.darkcontinents.com

Book Design by John Prescott
Cover Photograph by Ena
Cover Manipulation by John Prescott
Author Photo by Wendy Unsworth

ISBN 978-0-983-62451-6

PRINTED IN AUSTRALIA, UNITED STATES OF AMERICA, UNITED KINGDOM

Previously Published in

Scale Hall - *Where the Heart Is,* Gray Friar Press, 2010

The Elms Morecambe - *Spectrum Collection*, Dark Continents Publishing, Inc., 2010

Table of Contents

Dedication

To the lights and hearts of my life: Wendy, who wishes her house was quiet, and Benjamin who helps me keep it noisy. Without them, there would be no stories worth telling.

Do you live in a haunted house? Have you ever been to a place and had an experience you cannot explain? Do you have a story to tell? Serious researcher wants to hear from you. Must be prepared to go on record.

No timewasters.

Tel: 01524 500501 ext 23 and leave a message.

Nakata 1: University Office

There were one hundred fifty-eight messages when he accessed his voice-mail.

Most of them Nakata deleted after listening to them once, although he noted for each one the kind of message it was, wondering if there was some additional research he could gather from this, about people's responses to the sort of request he had made. Seventy-one he listed as 'positions', instructions or questions for him, mentioning particular buildings or places. Had he thought about the castle? The prison? He should visit the hairdressers just down the road from where the caller lived, because every time the caller went there for a haircut, they felt uncomfortable. It wasn't even that these people were wrong, he thought, it was simply that this wasn't what he was after. Twenty-nine hadn't left contact details ('anonymous'), and a further forty-four were 'nearlies', people who knew someone who'd had the kind of experience he wanted to record but hadn't had one themselves: *my grandfather had a funny experience, my mum told me there was a place, my wife said, my husband, my child, a neighbour, my friend.* Eleven were 'impressionists', people making ghostly noises, *whoooooo* and booming, hollow laughter. He looked meditatively at the columns of crosshatched lines, columns with their whimsical titles, and added them. One hundred and fifty-five.

That left three.

Three stories that might be useful, where the people had left numbers for him to call back, nervous voices saying, *I heard something* and *There's something that happened to me that might be what you're after* and *I've seen something.* He noted their numbers and names, sitting at his desk with his notebook open. Three. Not a lot, but it was a start. There might be more to-morrow, the day after, the day after that; the advert was due to run for the rest of the week and all of the following week, and if he got three each day that was more than forty in total, and surely some of them would be usable? He added an extra column to his table: Potential.

Taking a deep breath, Nakata dialled the first number.

The Elms, Morecambe

Nakata shifted; the cafe's seats weren't exactly uncomfortable, but the angle of their upright made his back twinge. Across from him the man, Wisher, reacted to the shift by glancing up from his coffee and then back down again. Nakata waited, letting Wisher find his own timings and securities, suspecting that any pressure would lead to the man closing down into silence.

"It's closed," Wisher said eventually. "I don't suppose it matters anymore."

"Take your time," said Nakata. Beyond Wisher's shoulder, the cafe's large front windows had grown a skin of condensation across their insides, and the world beyond had become a loose morass of grey smears through which darker shapes sometimes passed. In the last week the weather had soured, becoming cold and wet. If he could have seen it, he knew that the sea beyond the wide pavements and strip of beach would be bucking and unsettled. "You know I have to record this? That you need to go on the record for this to be any use to me?"

"Yes," said Wisher, his voice thin. "Like I said, it doesn't matter. Not now."

"It might," said Nakata.

"No," said Wisher, and this time Nakata didn't respond, understanding that Wisher was speaking only to something within himself.

"There's a hotel," said Wisher after a few moments. "Or, at least, there was. It was the best one in town until The Midland reopened, but it shut last year. The building's still there; they started work on converting it to apartments, but then the money ran out and they stopped. It's covered in scaffolding. It's a shame. I mean, it's not the most attractive of buildings, but still." He broke off, eyes leaping up to Nakata's face and then immediately dropping away again. Whatever had happened to this man, it had exhausted him, Nakata saw: the flesh under his eyes was bruised with tiredness, and the expression on his face was one of hopelessness, all the confidence leached out of him.

"It was a nice place," he finally said.

"What was it called?" asked Nakata. "The more information you can give me, the better."

"The Elms," said Wisher after a pause in which the indecision played across his face. "It was nice, old fashioned but kept nicely, you know?"

"Yes."

"The members of staff were good, attentive without being pushy. The head waiter was Hungarian, Polish, something like that; he'd been there as long as I can remember, always polite, good at his job. He could do that thing when he poured champagne, making it look like he was being careless and making it fizz up but knowing just when to stop so that the bubbles came up past the rim of the glass and looked like they were about to spill over, but they never did. It always made Julie smile when he did that. Funny, the things you remember, isn't it?"

"Yes," said Nakata again. He checked his dictaphone, tiny and black on the table between them. It should be picking up Wisher's voice easily enough; the sound of the cafe was still low. It was midmorning, midweek, and the other customers were mostly older couples. The air was damp with the exhalations of rain and sweat from their clothes and coats and skin, and was gently poaching in the heat from the small kitchen. Three umbrellas lay by the door, inverted and dripping like wounded crabs.

"It served good food, which was why we went, mostly. Sunday lunches, good roast dinners. We went for Christmas one year, when Julie didn't feel like cooking. That was the Christmas before she died," said Wisher, his voice empty. "But we never stayed there overnight. We'd never needed to; we lived nearby, so it was only a short taxi ride away. It was just a place we liked.

"Then my daughter decided to get married, and she decided to have the reception in The Elms." Wisher let out a long, loose sigh that sounded as though it was attached to him with threads that twitched as they emerged, pulling it into a new, uneven shape. "This was a year or so after Julie died, and she only chose the place because I liked it, I'm sure. I told her she shouldn't pick it because of me, if they wanted to go somewhere else, somewhere more modern. She said no, The Elms was where she wanted her wedding reception to be. I should've tried harder."

Nakata finished his coffee, waiting for Wisher to continue. The message the man had left on Nakata's voicemail had been like this, elliptical, unclear, as though he was skirting the real meaning of what he wanted to say, harrying at its edges but refusing to tackle it head on.

"I decided to stay there, rather than go home, on the night of the wedding. Lots of family and friends were staying, so I thought it'd be nice to spend time over breakfast with them on the Sunday morning. If I'm honest, I wasn't sure how I'd be if I went home after. Without Julie, I mean. Without her to share it with. Besides, the rumours that The Elms was going to close were pretty strong by that point, and I wanted to say I'd stayed there, even if it was just once. It felt important. Does that make sense?"

"Yes," said Nakata. *My role here is validation*, he thought briefly. *To hear him and tell him things are okay, that the story is real even if the facts turn out not to be, no matter what the story is. To let him know that someone believes him.*

"It was a lovely day, even without Julie," said Wisher after another pause, as though marshalling himself. "Meg, that's my daughter, she looked so beautiful and Oscar, her husband, he's a good man and they were so happy. Everyone enjoyed themselves, and The Elms was excellent. The food was cooked just right and served properly, all the tables of guests getting their food at the same time so that no one was waiting for their starters as some people got their main courses. I think that's important, it shows that the restaurant, caterers, whatever, are taking it seriously, don't you? I'm glad, even with everything that's happened since, that I had that day. That Meg had her day, and I could be there with her.

"Anyway, even though I enjoyed myself, I thought I'd have an early night. The disco was loud, and I was starting to miss Julie more and more, to wish she was there to see Meg so happy, and it was upsetting me. She was always better at that kind of thing than I was, and I didn't want to sit in the corner and get maudlin and upset, spoil Meg and Oscar's night, have people see me make a show of myself, so I said my goodbyes and I went to my room."

Nakata shifted again. He was wet from the seafront rain, the damp probing around his crotch and his shoulders, warm and uncomfortable in the clinging, moist atmosphere of the cafe.

"I'd got a twin room," said Wisher, "and I was just sitting down on one of the beds with a cup of tea and watching the news, trying not to miss Julie, when there was a knock at the door. I was a bit surprised, really. I'd gone to bed early compared to most, but it was still late for visiting, and I didn't want anyone trying to persuade me to go back downstairs. I was still dressed, except for my shoes and tie and jacket, but I didn't want to talk to anyone, not then. I just wanted to sit and be quiet and drink my tea and watch what was happening in the world and try to enjoy the last bit of the day, but whoever it was knocked again. I only answered, in the end, because I suddenly thought it might be Meg and that she might need something.

When I opened the door, there was a young woman, a girl really, standing there. She was very neatly dressed, in a black skirt and a white blouse, and she had her hair tied back off her face. She wasn't wearing any makeup, and she looked very young. I didn't recognise her from the wedding, so I said "Yes?" and I must have sounded angry because she took a step back from the door as if she wanted to get out of my reach. I said "Yes?" again, and she said, "Can I turn your sheets, sir?"

This time, Wisher looked Nakata in the eye, hunching his shoulders up as though to protect his neck, the expectation of disbelief clear in his expression. "It sounds stupid, doesn't it? 'Can I turn your sheets, sir?'"

"No," said Nakata. "It doesn't. What did the girl look like? Her clothes, I mean?"

"Normal. Plain," said Wisher. "But that's not what you're asking is it, not really? You mean, could I tell she was a ghost? No, I couldn't. She wasn't see-through, her clothes weren't old fashioned, and she wasn't wearing a bonnet that made me think of the Victorians or the Edwardians or whoever. She just looked like a normal girl, woman. I'm not stupid, I know that it's not usual for hotel staff to offer to turn people's sheets back these days, but I just thought it was something The Elms did, like, oh I don't know, like a selling point, you know? 'Little old-world touches to make your stay more pleasurable'," he intoned, and then stopped.

"I wasn't going to let her in," he said after swallowing the last of his coffee. "It had been such a nice day, but it had been so busy and I'd been so nervous making my speech and then talking to everyone. Most of them hadn't seen me since Julie had died, except maybe at the funeral, and they were all asking me how I was *doing*, how I was *coping*, and I'd been saying 'Yes, yes, fine, thanks, it's hard but I'm getting there' or variations of it all day, even though that wasn't really true, not really, and I just wanted a little peace and quiet with no people around me before I went to sleep. I even opened my mouth to tell her no, I wasn't interested, but she looked so small and miserable and I couldn't do it."

"I'm not sure I understand," said Nakata.

"Neither do I!" cried out Wisher suddenly, startling Nakata. The couple at the next table looked around, but Wisher appeared not to have noticed. "She wasn't doing anything. She was just standing in the corridor, her face white because the light was right above her, just standing there, and she was sad, I could *feel* it, so sad. It was like there was something hanging around her, something I couldn't see but I could feel it just by the way she was standing and I don't know, maybe it was because I'd had such a good day, been with all those happy people, or maybe because her sadness felt a little like my sadness, as though she was missing someone or something too, and I didn't want to add to it, make her feel worse, so I didn't say no, I stood back from the door and said, 'Yes, come in'." He took another of those loose, twitched breaths and then said loudly, "And she came in."

People at a number of the other tables were looking at them now, the staff behind the counter peering towards them. Wisher dropped his face into his hands, his elbows on the table. One was in a puddle of spilled coffee, Nakata saw, but he said nothing; Wisher was sobbing, near-silent and hoarse. Nakata rose and went to the counter, purchasing two more coffees then returning to his seat slowly with the drinks, giving Wisher time to recover himself. The cafe was darker, he noticed, as though the lights were struggling against the out-of-season atmosphere. The condensation coating the inside of the windows was thicker, occasionally breaking to roll down the glass in fat, heavy rivulets. Looking around, he saw that one of the people at a nearby table was also crying, her companion stroking her arm gently. Near the door, a young girl was trying to calm a fractious child, bouncing him on her knee. The child refused to be comforted, was red-faced and grizzling, his eyes screwed shut and his glistening tongue emerging from his mouth like some pink worm tasting the air.

"She came in," said Wisher when his sobs had subsided, "and went to the middle of the room. The bed I'd been sitting on was clear, but the other one had my jacket on it and a bag with my toilet things and a book and clothes for the next day, and when she saw them, her shoulders fell. I was standing behind her, and I saw them, saw her shoulders drop so that they were sloped down, like the bed with things on was the most upsetting thing she'd ever seen. She shuffled, taking these little slow steps like an old woman, went to the other bed and peeled the sheets back from under the pillows, getting one corner out and folding it back so that I could easily pull them back to get in, and then she looked at the other bed again and her shoulders just sort of slumped even further. I can't even explain it, not properly, but it was so upsetting, like seeing a child cry, and I couldn't stand it. I think I said something like, 'I'll move the bag, don't worry'. She looked at me, and the look on her face was so grateful, like I'd given her a gift, not just offered to shift my overnight bag.

"I put the bag on the floor and picked my jacket up, then she came and turned the sheets back, just like on the other bed. Afterwards she said, 'Thank you, sir', and went to the door. As she went past me, I patted her arm, just to say thank you, to try to cheer her up, and she turned to me and smiled and oh, it was the most awful smile! It was like she was trying not to cry, that a terrible wrong had been done to her and she was putting a brave face on it, but couldn't really do it and the misery she felt was just there, under the surface of her skin and about to burst out. I didn't know what to say, whether she wanted something from me, was waiting for something else, but she just said, 'Thank you, sir,' and went out. 'Thank you, sir.'"

Wisher took a mouthful of his coffee; his hands shook as he lifted the cup to his mouth, Nakata saw. He let out another of those disjointed breaths and then said, "By the next morning, I'd persuaded myself that she hadn't really looked like that. She didn't like her job, was pissed off with having to work on a Saturday night turning the sheets of fat middle-aged men who patted her on the arm, and I'd misread the expression on her face because of my own confusion; being happy and sad and lonely and not wanting to see anyone getting all mixed up in me, making me see things that weren't there. I had a nice breakfast with some of my friends and family, made promises to keep in touch, and then went to check out. I wanted to get home by then; I'd had enough of being away. I just wanted to be somewhere that was completely mine, was empty, so that I could relax, where there was no need to smile or pretend or be anything but me.

"As I checked out, I said something about the girl to the man behind the counter, just that she'd done a good job or something, but he looked at me as though he didn't know what I was talking about. I said it again, that the girl who came to turn my sheets had been very good or something. I don't know, I thought that if she was told that one of the guests had said something nice about her, she might feel a bit better, be a bit less upset or angry or whatever, but the man behind the counter just looked at me again like I was talking gibberish. The head waiter, the Hungarian, though, he was standing nearby and he must have heard because he said, 'Oh ho ho, so you have had a midnight visit?' I remember that he said, 'oh ho ho', because I'd never heard anyone else say it before. 'Oh ho ho', like some great big Santa, and he's smiling at me like it's some sort of joke. I think I said something like, 'Pardon', and he said, 'The mysterious chambermaid! Did you not know? She has been visiting people here for years, knocking on the doors of guests and offering to turn their sheets or clean their shoes.'

"'Who is she?' I asked, and he said, 'We do not know. She comes at night every now and again. She causes no trouble and she leaves when people send her away. Often it is a long time between her visits, or people do not tell us because it is such a silly thing, is it not? She is The Elms' ghost!' I thought he was, you know, joking, that it was a practical joke, but even though he was laughing as he said it, I realised he was being serious.

"A ghost?" I asked.

"Our very own, the only one we have!" he said. 'But harmless. She goes and does not come back, whoever she is. I have been here years, more than I care to remember, and in all that time she has never bothered anyone. She asks, is sent away and comes not again!' He should have sounded comical, with his funny accent, but somehow he didn't. 'I thought everyone knew of her,' he said, 'our little sad girl. Tell me, how miserable did she look when you sent her away?' 'I didn't,' I said. 'I let her turn the sheets, and she went after she'd done.'

"At that, the Hungarian gave a big grin and said, 'So our poor girl has done her job, yes? Good girl!' and then he was shaking my hand and asking me if everything had been good enough and walking with me to my car. He was so good, so careful, even how he walked, you know? Precise. Neat. I wish I could remember his name, just calling him 'The Hungarian' sounds so dismissive. It may not even be right; he might have been a Pole or from one of those countries that have been invented these past few years and that keep fighting each other. Eastern Europe, anyway."

Nakata moved again, rolling the base of his spine forward to stop it knotting. He was sweating with the trapped heat of the cafe now, his sweat mixing with the moisture seeping through his clothes to form a layer that was clammy against his skin. Wisher groaned and lowered his head again, saying something that Nakata missed. "You need to say it louder, please," he said, "so that the recorder catches it. I have to have it on record."

"Yes," said Wisher. "I said 'It doesn't matter'. I mean, which country he was from, it doesn't matter, not now. He's not important, I never saw him again. I only went back to The Elms one more time.

"About a week later, I saw in the local paper that The Elms had closed a couple of days after Meg's wedding. The staff members were told first thing one morning and then made to work their shifts that day. There was a 70th birthday held in the hotel that day, if I remember right, which I thought was cruel. It must have been hard for them to work that birthday party, to be cheerful and serve the guests like nothing had happened and all the while knowing that they'd just lost their jobs. After all, whatever problems the hotel had, the service was good, and I wondered what had happened to them. To the Hungarian. I even thought about the girl in the night, but I'd pretty much decided that the Hungarian had been joking. Perhaps he'd just thought of it on the spur of the moment, or maybe it was a regular thing they did. It seemed a bit childish, I suppose, but not harmful. Not harmful.

"And then she came again.

"I was asleep, in my own bed, alone as ever since Julie died, but I think I remember being mostly happy before I went to bed that night. As happy as I got, anyway. I wish I could remember it better, really, say that the night had something to mark it out and make it different, but it didn't." He gave a laugh, explosive and bitter, and then said, "After all, it's not often you find a ghost in your bedroom, is it?"

"No," said Nakata. "It's not. What happened?"

"Have you got children?" asked Wisher, suddenly.

"No," said Nakata, suddenly, strangely, conscious that his wedding ring finger was bare. Wisher was spinning the ring on his own finger.

"When they're young, sometimes kids will come in and lean over you. They don't make any sound, they don't touch: if they're trying very hard, they'll even hold their breath so that they don't disturb you that way. Somehow, though, you know they're there; it's like you can sense them without knowing quite how. Maybe it's the love you can feel, if you're lucky enough to have kids who love you. Well, that's what happened at first; I woke up because there was someone standing over me, bending down, their face not far from mine, close enough to kiss me but not breathing, not touching me. I thought I was dreaming, remembering Meg when she was a girl and she'd creep in and see how long it would take for me and her mum to wake up.

"I opened my eyes, and as I did I remembered that Meg was older now, married and living with Oscar, that Julie was gone, had been for over a year, and suddenly I was panicking. If someone was in the room, then they weren't supposed to be. The room was dark. I've never been able to sleep if there was even a bit of light, but I could see that there was someone on the other side of the room, a darker patch in the shadows. They weren't near me, weren't bending over me like I'd thought, but there was a definite shape, a person, and even though I couldn't see, I knew that they were looking at me, staring at me.

"I wanted to scream, but I was frozen. I'm not a brave man; I haven't ever been one for fighting or even arguments, so screaming seemed like the best bet, trying to frighten them away or startle them, but before I could, they spoke.

"'Turn your sheets, sir?'"

"It was so stupid that it stopped me from screaming. It was the girl from The Elms. I recognised the voice, and I think that that was worse than a burglar in a funny sort of way. I remembered the Hungarian saying 'our little sad girl', and I think I spoke, said something inane like 'What' or 'Pardon,' and she said again, 'Turn your sheets, sir?' and came forward so that I could see her face. She was smiling, but it was a smile like the one she'd given me as she left my room in The Elms, like it was perched on top of a great heap of unhappiness and misery, was slithering around and trying to hold it all in. She looked grey in the darkness, and her eyes were so hopeful, so *desperate*, and I did scream then, and scrambled back across the bed, the same one I'd shared with Julie. How I wished she was there to tell me it was a dream, that I was being silly, but she wasn't. There was just me and this girl who I knew was a ghost--not because the Hungarian had told me--but because the unhappiness was coming off her in waves. I could feel it, so thick, and no one could be that unhappy and be alive."

Nakata watched as Wisher slumped down across the table. It was like watching the air being let out of a balloon, as though Wisher had held it all inside, stiffening in him like souring milk until there was nothing else and now that it was out, he could collapse. The only reason that his head didn't hit the table was that it was cradled in hands that were shaking badly now, the fingers spread out and pressing into the scalp that glistened pinkly from under the thinning hair.

"I fell out of the bed and onto the floor, and when I did, she came right to the side of the bed and she gripped my duvet and shook it, straightening it then folding back the top of it so that it was ready to get into. I'd banged my head when I fell and had stopped screaming, and I didn't start again. I watched as she shook the pillow I'd been lying on, plumping it up and laying it against the headboard, then she smiled at me, the same, awful, thankful smile, and backed away into the corner, and as she went she sort of blended with the shadows and then she was gone.

"I couldn't move at first, terrified that she might come back as soon as I did, but eventually I started to get cold. I couldn't get back into the bed, wouldn't, so instead I went downstairs. I must have looked like a thief, because I didn't even run, I *scurried* downstairs, trying to be small and insignificant and not be noticed by anyone. Anything. I sat in my lounge with all the lights on until the sun came up and then I opened the curtains, and even then the room didn't feel bright enough. I wanted all the shadows gone from the corners so that I could feel normal, but it didn't work.

"Had I dreamed her? Hallucinated? I didn't know, but I do know she had felt real, actual, that my memories of her were the memories of something that had actually happened. Maybe that's how mad people think, I don't know.

A real ghost. Jesus." Wisher sat up again, looking across at Nakata. Nakata had never actually seen anyone square their shoulders before, but Wisher did so now. "I'm not lying or mad, Mr Nakata. The girl was in my bedroom."

"I know," said Nakata. "I believe you. It sounds as though it was terrifying."

"Terrifying," repeated Wisher slowly. "Yes. Yes, it was terrifying, and so was finding her in the kitchen when I went through to make myself a coffee.

"She was at the kitchen, doing my dishes, washing the plates as though it was the most normal thing in the world. I stopped in the doorway, and it was as though some huge hand had grabbed my heart in my chest. It was partly the fear of her, this stranger in my house, but also it was the feelings again, the sense of loss and desperation coming off her. It filled the room, and I suddenly missed Julie again, and wished that I could die, just fall dead there between the kitchen and the hallway so that I could go where she'd gone and join her."

Nakata nodded, understanding what Wisher meant. An image came to him, unbidden, of Amy, lost to him for almost three years now. The knowledge that he would only ever see her smile in old photographs and in his memory hit him hard, harder than it had in months. He could smell her, taste her memory, and the missing her welled up in him with bitter force. He started to speak, but his voice cracked. Wisher, hearing it, looked across at him, grinning broadly and without humour. "Horrible, isn't it?" he said.

"She was everywhere with me after that, this girl. All the time, waking me up with offers to turn my sheets, being ahead of me in the rooms I went into even if she had been in the room I'd just left only moments before, asking if I wanted some menial task doing. Sometimes I'd agree, and she'd disappear when she'd done it, but more often I would ignore her, and she'd stand in the corner staring at me, waiting for me to tell her to do something. I tried to tell her to go, to leave me alone, but she wouldn't; she'd just stand there with a look on her face like I'd kicked her, like I'd betrayed her and that it was exactly what she'd expected.

"At first I was scared, *terrified*, but soon the fear faded. It sounds silly, doesn't it? That having a ghost with you all the time could ever not be frightening, but in the end there wasn't much to be frightened *of*. She was just always there, always, always trailing after me or being up ahead of me, looking at me as though I was the answer to her problems. Even when I went out, she would appear, standing behind me in shops or next to me in lifts. She once spent the whole of a car journey sitting on the back seat of my car so that I could almost see her in the mirror every time I looked. Nothing I did or said seemed to make a difference, she was just there, whether I wanted her or not.

"Eventually, I went back to The Elms. I'm not sure what I hoped for, maybe that she might see the building and somehow be stuck back into it, but I knew as soon as I got there it wouldn't work. I could feel the difference as I stood in the car park; whatever had made the building more than just bricks, wood, and glass had gone. It was covered in scaffolding, the windows were boarded up and there were chains through the door handles on the main doors, but it was more than that. The *life* had gone from it. All the while I was looking at it, I could see her out of the corner of my eye, standing by the car. Even in the shadows of the falling night, I could feel her misery. Her shoulders were down, her head bowed, and I suddenly had the most awful thought: what if I'd brought this on myself? What if, by showing her some kindness, by acknowledging her, I'd somehow given her the power to come with me, that when The Elms closed she'd followed the last person who had been nice to her? Had I given her some hope, however small, and anchored her to me?"

Wisher fell silent. The cafe's breathing went on around him, the child still squalling and the woman at the nearby table still weeping quietly, her companion comforting her. Nakata took another mouthful of his coffee and found that it had gone cold, the liquid cloying, clinging to his teeth and coating his tongue tastelessly. He wanted to speak, but wasn't sure what he could say, thinking instead about Amy. She would have known what to do or say, had always been so much better than him at making people feel better. Wisher, his features haggard and his skin the colour of whey, saw Nakata looking across the table at him and said, "I went home. What else could I do?

"I think I could even have got used to my personal ghost, whoever she was, but for the feelings."

"What feelings?"

"It was all about her, like a cloud," said Wisher, apparently ignoring the question. Now, he looked at Nakata fully, meeting his gaze and smiling a terrible, rictus smile. "Misery. Unhappiness. Loneliness. It wasn't just the look on her face or the way she stood or the sound of her, it was something else. You could feel it, all about her, and it soaked into the walls and the floor of my home, like cigarette smoke will do if there's a smoker in the house, staining everything. Whoever this girl was, whatever she'd been through when she was alive, it had left her so terribly sad, and her sadness was contagious. I'd never had many visitors, not since Julie died anyway, but even Meg and Oscar stopped coming to my house. Meg told me she thought I should get out more, that the house was full of old memories and it wasn't healthy for me to be there all the time, but she was wrong, it wasn't the memories that were unhealthy; they were the only thing keeping me going. If I could remember Julie, remember Meg and Julie together when Meg was little, remember the Christmases we'd had there and the birthdays, and how Julie smelled and felt when we hugged, then the blackness that surrounded the girl never quite overwhelmed me and I could keep it at bay. Even when I went out in public, the girl was there, always hovering at the edges of crowds or just behind me so that I could see her in the reflections in shop windows but never when I turned around to look at her directly. Thank Christ I'd retired after Julie died, I don't know how I'd have coped at work on top of everything else, having to act as though everything was fine when all the time she'd have been in the corner of the office or standing behind people at meetings and looking at me. And it wasn't just me; if I went somewhere in public, she'd be in the room with me and I think people would see her but would ignore her, move around her, but after a while you'd see them get caught by it as well. They'd *sag*, look miserable, stop laughing. Eventually I stopped going out unless I had to."

"Did you talk to anyone about her, tell anyone what was happening?"

"Who? What would I tell them?" asked Wisher, his voice cold. Steam from the coffee maker behind the counter danced above their heads for a moment before dissipating. More condensation broke on the windows, rolling down the glass in long strings like wounds that healed almost as soon as they were opened, scabbing over with more grey, misting skin. Nakata felt tired, emotionally worn, as though he'd been in the cafe for hours or days rather than simply part of the morning. The sounds of the child crying were becoming wearing now, the comforting sounds from its mother irritating; the people at the next table had settled into a routine of tears, conversation, tears, which Nakata found equally hard to hear. Shadows gathered around his feet and under the tables nearby, pools of dirty light through which the floor glimmered, the tiles ill-formed and murky. He looked again at the recorder, at the time counter rolling implacably onwards, and thought again of Amy and the way she had of making the world feel brighter, lighter. "Who would I tell?" asked Wisher again, and Nakata couldn't answer him. Instead, he asked another question.

"What did you do? To stop it, I mean?"

"What did I do to stop it?" repeated Wisher, grimacing. "What could I do? Nothing."

"Nothing?"

"Nothing. I wondered about talking to a priest, but what would I say? That I was being haunted by the ghost of a sad, lonely girl who tried to help me but made me feel terrible? So no, I did nothing."

"So how did you stop her haunting you?"

"I didn't. She's sitting at one of the tables at the back of the cafe now, staring at me."

Nakata started and began to turn but Wisher lunged across the table and gripped his shoulders, saying, "Don't!

"That feeling you have, now, of misery? That little wave of sadness you felt before? You remembered someone important to you, yes? Someone who's died or you don't see any more, and the memory made you sad? Yes? That's *nothing* to how it feels when she's with you all the time. You cannot acknowledge her, please, because if you turn to her, see her, *believe in her*, she may come to you when I'm gone."

Nakata tried to twist again to see her, see the ghost in the cafe that might prove once and for all the things he had argued for so long, but Wisher gripped his shoulder more tightly. "I've not told you this because I think you can help," he said, "or to shift my burden to you, but because I want it said before it's too late. I don't see anyone anymore; don't see Meg or Oscar because I don't want them exposed to her, don't want her dogging them like she has me, making everything in their lives cold and miserable the way she has mine." He lifted his other hand to Nakata's face, placing it almost tenderly along his cheek so that he couldn't turn any further around. The child screamed, desolate, and the person at the next table wept openly. Nakata struggled against Wisher's grip, thinking of Amy, of what seeing the dead girl might mean for Amy and for him, but still couldn't move.

"I'll go soon, there's nothing more to tell. I've tried to photograph her and record her, but it doesn't work, there's nothing there when I check the pictures or the recording. I'm sure other people can see her, sometimes, but they don't know what she is, don't realise, and I'm glad. Wherever I go, she comes along and she brings these feelings with her. I can see it, see people suddenly remember something sad, see their moods drop, watch them as they suddenly think of something that hurts them, and they change in front of me, all around me. Don't look around, please. Don't look for her, or at her. Please. *Please*."

Wisher let go of Nakata and stood, saying, "I have very little time left anyway. Meg and Oscar, they're happy, and Julie's waiting for me, I hope. This poor girl, she needs to belong to me. I don't know why, but maybe when I'm gone, she'll go on, too. Maybe she'll realise that she doesn't have to keep hold of all this unhappiness, all this grief, and she can be free, too. I hope so. I hope this is useful, Mr Nakata, I truly do."

Nakata watched as Wisher walked to the door. There was a rustle of cloth as someone went past him, and in the corner of his eye he caught a glimpse of someone in a dark skirt and white blouse go past. The feelings of loss, of missing Amy, rose sharply in him, hard and taut and painful. Wisher turned briefly and nodded back at him and then left. A moment later Nakata watched a girl's back as she, too, left. As the door clicked shut behind her, the infant in the corner gave a grizzled burp and stopped squalling. Its mother said, "That's better, baby," and there was tired relief in her voice. The child giggled suddenly, high and bright. At the next table, the woman had stopped crying and was smiling across the table at her companion.

Wisher's blurred shape passed across the front of the cafe windows, indistinct and grey on the far side of the weeping glass, and a step behind him, a smaller, darker shape followed.

Nakata 2: Train and beyond

"My son disappeared."

A voice in the digital ether at first, responding not to the advert in the personal columns but to Nakata's second approach, placing the same advert in the 'wanted' sections of various local papers. "My son disappeared." The man wouldn't meet him anywhere near the university, instead demanding that Nakata came to his home. It meant a train journey to Manchester and then another out along one of the branch lines, the city's modern gleam replaced initially with greenery and then with industrial architecture left, unsupported, to carry the weight of its history. Rows of terraced homes appeared, spreading in ranks up the hillsides above the railway cuttings, ramshackle factories and shopping centres dotted among them like the glowering, crouched figures of gargoyles on cathedral roofs. He used the time on the train to type up what he'd found so far; it wasn't much, and Tidyman would likely be unhappy. Still, that couldn't be helped; Nakata had told Tidyman from the beginning that this was almost certainly a fool's errand. "Then call me a fool," Tidyman had said, and had set Nakata running with all his expenses covered.

Although it wasn't raining, the streets were wet when Nakata alighted from the train, their surfaces slick and glittering in sunlight that seemed tired and weak. He started walking to the address he had been given, following the printed map and checking each street name carefully as he passed. Some of the streets had no signs, and he had to guess which ones they were. Others had signs that were battered and faded, their letters lost unless he stood right next to them. It was further than he'd realised, and he became aware as he walked of how people looked at him as he passed, not exactly unfriendly but wary. *It's not the cast of my eyes nor my skin, it's just that I'm new, an unknown*, he thought. An unknown who was clearly unsure of his place, following a map printed from a website, and he wondered about his safety and if he should have taken a taxi from the station and hated himself for falling into the traps of casual racism and for making assumptions about the attitudes and intentions of the people he saw.

Finally, he came to the right street and found the house and knocked, but no one answered. He felt exposed on the street, an easy target for. . .what? He didn't know. Ridicule, perhaps. Attack, maybe. Had the man decided against talking after all, but not let Nakata know?

Nakata knocked again, harder, wondering if the man had gone away. *My son disappeared.*

He was about to knock a third time when the door swung open, and the old man appeared. He was exactly as Nakata had imagined him: grizzled, his eyebrows thick and jutting from his head in tangles, his hair short across his pate, his clothes old but neat. He looked worn out, but his handshake was firm and his voice, when he spoke, was as it had been on the voicemail, gruff and throaty in a way that Nakata associated with people who didn't speak often, ex-smokers, drinkers.

"I've never shown anyone this," said the old man, Crosby, after ushering Nakata into the lounge and gesturing for him to sit on a threadbare sofa. "It came a few days after the last time he was seen by anyone. I never showed anyone, because I always wanted to keep it secret. I didn't want people to think he'd gone funny, but now there's no point in keeping it secret. I wanted to protect Dominic and Terri, but there's no reason to now, she's found someone else and moved on. I haven't seen either of them for a year." Crosby's voice cracked a little during the last sentence, and Nakata watched him swallow, hard, before continuing. "His mother's long gone now, so it can't hurt her either, and he's beyond caring. If this is right, he died a hero, if it's not then. . .well, then it doesn't matter either way. There's only me left to care, and there's nothing can be said that'll hurt me more than I hurt already, if the truth be told."

As he spoke, Crosby picked up a large brown envelope, spun it slowly in his hands, and then handed it across to Nakata. Nakata looked at the older man, who nodded and then opened it, upending it so that the contents, a stack of photocopies stapled together into a fat sheaf, fell into his hand. Looking closely, he saw that all of them were covered in tight, small handwritten lines.

"My son's last letter to me, just before he disappeared," said Crosby. "Well, a copy. You aren't having the original. It's not a suicide note, before you ask, and I have no idea if what he wrote was true. Part of me wants it to be, because then maybe he disappeared for the best of reasons, and part of me doesn't want it to be, because if it is we may all be damned. Read it; make your own mind up."

Nakata started to look at the first sheet, but Crosby leaned over and said, "No. You take it away and read it somewhere else, not here. I can't answer your questions, wouldn't anyway, and I don't know what it means. You go back to where you came from and read it. I've written all the details, names and dates and the like, on the back sheet for you so you can check what details you can from that. Go and read it somewhere away from me." His hand fell to the paper and he looked at it for a moment, sadness etched over his face. "Lord, but he was a wordy bugger, always was, even when he was writing, but he was mine and I loved him. My son, he disappeared, and I miss him every day."

As Nakata left, Crosby began crying, and they sounded like old, familiar tears.

The Merry House, Scale Hall

Dad

I'm sorry for writing to you like this, that I couldn't ring, but I don't know what else to do. You're not any more likely to believe me than anyone else, I don't suppose, but you're my dad and I love you and I want you to know what's happening and I know I can trust you. Christ, it seems like madness, now I come to write it. Sitting here in the bright sunlight, in my garden, watching Dominic play in his paddling pool, it seems beyond madness, not even an insanity, but a preposterousness, a thing of fantasy, but it is not. I only have to watch my son to understand that, to see that, every few minutes he stops playing and looks towards the garden gate, looks beyond it at something I cannot see, and I am reminded of the truth of these words.

There is another world below this one, a world inhabited by ghosts and demons and all the things that we have lost that we should not find again. I have heard it described as Hell, this other place, and I used to think that this was nothing more than a metaphor for human frailty, a kind of poetry to make sense of the world, but I know now that it is not. That world beneath us exists, is real, and we are protected from it by a skin that we walk upon every moment, unknowingly stepping over things we cannot hope to understand, intelligences and lusts and desires that are as alien to us as the emotions of bees or the love of snakes. When we walk across the surface of this other world, we are protected from falling through to it by luck and the lightness of our step and the strength of the skin where we step. Most of the time it is strong, stretching and reshaping itself to accommodate our footfalls. I think that sometimes it wears thin, and in these worn places, we might get brief visions of the things that exist below us, see ghosts and monsters peering up from their sunless caverns, hear frantic breath echoing from that other place. We may even feel their touch in the prickle of our own skin and the clench of our bellies, but they are harmless, these things that appear, these mere nightmares and dreams and pictures.

In other places, though, the skin can rupture.

Where there are ruptures, the things that live below can escape upwards, can send questing tendrils into this world and draw back what they catch. These ruptures never truly heal, they merely scab over, crusted and dark and weeping. Around these open wounds the nightmares can become real, the dreams grow flesh, and pieces of our world can be caught and taken into the lost places beneath our feet. People can be caught, can be lost. It has happened here in Scale Hall. It will happen again.

There is nothing special about Scale Hall; you know that, you've been here. I've checked, tried to find something that might explain what's happened, but I can't. Scale Hall is a small suburb, located roughly halfway between Lancaster and Morecambe. It was originally little more than a collection of industrial sites serving nearby factories, a tiny part of the industrial and rail chains that stretched across the country in the period between the wars, and until the second quarter of the twentieth century it had its own rail station (operated by the London and Midland company, I'm told – find the details, you once told me, and I've never forgotten that. Details, details, each one important, none to be lost). Did you know that it once had an airstrip, mostly used by the RAF for training flights, right on the site of the Grosvenor Park School? I didn't, but it's true – I keep wondering if there's any of it left beneath the school buildings. Probably not. It's funny, the things you think about when you're trying to avoid something, isn't it?

In recent years, the industrial landscape has changed, has declined, and Scale Hall has changed with it, becoming a commuter town serving Lancaster as well as the larger towns of the northwest. The biggest employers in Scale Hall now are the health service and Lancaster University, and it experiences the same problems with alcohol and anti-social behaviour as any other satellite suburb of an English town. It is anonymous, bordered by other anonymously identical conurbations, a place of boredom and domesticity, and its population rarely gets above two thousand people.

Since the 1960s, fourteen young children have disappeared from Scale Hall.

I have only been in the Merry House once.

Although the police didn't call for volunteers in the search, I don't imagine that anyone in Scale Hall didn't look for Sandra Cahill. On that first day, with the helicopter swooping overhead and its repeated announcement about the missing little girl wearing a Torrisholme School uniform drifting down from above us like spring blossoms, I suspect all of us checked the verges as we walked, looked at unaccompanied children with suspicion in our eyes, looked at *accompanied* children suspiciously, and the adults with them warily, and hoped to find her; I know I did. By lunchtime, ranks of black-clad police officers were walking the extended mudflats that the river exposed at low tide, whilst more of their number searched the college grounds and the Broadoak Garden Centre. By the second day, Scale Hall and the surrounding areas had been invaded by a silent, sombre army, methodically sweeping its way through the gardens and checking the outbuildings.

When she hadn't been found after a week, it was assumed that Sandra had been kidnapped. Early hopes that she had wandered off and become trapped in one of the Broadoak Garden Centre's many sheds or fallen and injured herself and would be found weak but alive, were fading. The police checked the entire length of the stream that runs down from the hills, sending remote cameras through the sections where it passes under roads before emptying into the Lune, and they dragged the Lune estuary itself. Platoons of searchers crawled over the Salt Ayre landfill, opening bags and sending sniffer dogs across the mounds of detritus, but they found nothing.

Scale Hall doesn't have much CCTV, but one camera in the Lancaster and Morecambe College grounds was found to have caught, in the far distance, a blurry image of a small child who might have been Sandra walking along the Torrisholme Road. She was unaccompanied, although at the edge of the image, ahead of her, a dark shape bobbed and jigged. No one who watched the film on the news seemed to be able to agree what the shape was; it was only visible for a few moments as the camera panned around, shifting and dark. Some people said it was a person dressed as a clown or a teddy bear, yet others said that it didn't resemble a person at all but a balloon on a string, or a kite. If the police had ideas about the shape, they kept them to themselves. You probably remember it; it wasn't that long ago. I think we spoke about it at the time, didn't we? What did you see on the film, Dad? What did anyone see?

Sandra's parents made tearful appearances on the nightly news, begging for the return of the daughter. The police were convinced that she had been enticed away somehow, groomed into leaving the safety of her home. They revealed that, over the days prior to her disappearance, Sandra's parents had found her on a number of occasions staring out through the slatted bars of her garden gate, an expression of rapt attention on her face, looking along the alleyway. What, or who, she was looking at wasn't known.

I knew Sandra, if only vaguely. She attended the same school as Dominic, although she was three years older than him. Her mother was one of the women I would say hello to in the playground, her daughter a little blonde thing whose hair tended to be tied in pigtails and who carried a *Hello Kitty* lunchbox and who always said hello to Dominic and me if she was stood near us. She seemed a sweet kid, one who apparently fell off the face of the world and left few traces of her passage behind. She had simply gone into the back garden of her home after her breakfast, where her mother watched her playing before going to get organised for the day ahead. Five minutes later, when she came back, Sandra was gone and the garden gate was swinging open. Those five minutes are, I imagine, terrible and endless in her mother's mind.

I don't know about everyone else, but it didn't take long before I stopped looking for Sandra as I walked Dominic to school, or walked the dogs, and began to think of her as dead, rotting somewhere out of sight and smell. If

I thought about her at all, it was as a flat, smiling image on a poster and of two distraught adults who looked lost and hopeless even as they cried and said their child's name over and over. Scale Hall and all the places around had been searched thoroughly, and she was not here; she was somewhere else, dead or as good as, in the possession of someone whose damaged personality and desires had turned them to evil, and if she was ever found it would be because that person had finished with her and discarded her. I wish I had been right; I wish that it had been a man, or death alone, that had found her.

I can't remember who told me it was called the Merry House, or when; possibly Andy or Lynda, our neighbours, during one of our Saturday barbeques that first summer after Terri and I moved here. I don't suppose it matters, really. It was simply the Merry House, an abandoned bungalow I passed every time I took the dogs down the ginnel that passes between the college and a row of houses and which connected the Morecambe and Torrisholme Roads. If it stood out all, it was only because of its abandonment; the bungalows around it were neatly tended and brightly lit homes, but from behind a warping wooden panel fence, the rear of the Merry House peered out at the alleyway in solitary decay.

The Merry House stands alone; the narrow gaps between it and the homes on either side are shadowed and thick. There are tiles missing from the roof, although not many; just enough to create an irregular patchwork of blackness against the slate angularity. Its windows and door are covered with perforated metal sheets, bolted to the brickwork to prevent entry, and the garden, long and thin, is overgrown. A narrow path stretches between the garden gate and the rear door, the concrete slabs discoloured and stained. There are three steps up from the garden to the door, their paintwork chipped and fading. An old greenhouse sits at the bottom of the garden, most of the panes broken and the plants inside it growing wild and furious, erupting out of the gaps where missing panes should be in a riot of green and brown and stems and thorns and leaves. The dogs don't like the Merry House and will not walk close to its bowing fence.

The night I saw the light from inside the Merry House, Sandra Cahill had been missing just over a week.

It was only a flickering glimmer, something pale behind the punctured metal cataracts of one of the two windows. It was late, almost midnight, and I was taking the dogs on their pre-sleep walk when I saw the light, and my first instinct was to think that someone had broken into the house. As I watched, the light passed behind one window and vanished, appearing a moment later in the other, and then vanished again. I tried to go closer to the fence, but the dogs resisted, pulling back and digging their feet into the muddy ground. The light reappeared behind the sheet covering the first window and seemed paler, almost translucent. I could hear nothing.

All the bungalows whose rears that look out into the alley belong to Norwood Drive, and at that time of night, the road was dark apart from the streetlights. The council had recently replaced the old orange sodium lights with new LED lamps, and as I tried to find the front of the Merry House, I passed through patches of light that were like the moon's glow made hard, but the strangest thing was, I couldn't find what I was looking for. When I got to the point on Norwood where I judged the building's front should be, I couldn't see it. Instead, I saw set after set of paired bungalows, partnered and content; nowhere could I find a lone building, and none looked abandoned. Every one I passed was neat, well-tended, loved. Inhabited.

Back in the alley, I found the abandoned house easily. The light was still flickering behind the screened windows, as though a cluster of fireflies was drifting around inside the old property. I wondered about calling the police, but to tell them what? That I had seen a light? Not even a light, but a glow? No. After everything that had happened this last week, I needed more than that, proof before calling down that army of patient, searching men and women. I tied the dogs to the college fence and walked over to the rotting gate, which was sagging out into the alley, the top hinge still holding it to the frame but the bottom long rusted away to nothing. I pulled at it, the wood damp and old against my skin, and it came open with a noise like teeth pulling from rotting gums. I managed to drag it open far enough so that I could squeeze through the gap and then I was, unknowing, stepping into a place where the skin of the world was torn, was raw and exposed and throbbing.

Light from the road and the college's security lamps seemed distant, spread out across the garden in irregular patterns. The building was larger than it looked from outside, as though peering over the fence at it had induced some odd foreshortening effect, and it was quiet, quieter even than the Scale Hall night. What sounds did reach me were muffled, as though I was hearing them through layers of cloth or from underwater. I peered back over the fence, calling a word to the dogs to calm them, and then started towards the house.

Hunched to my left, the greenhouse was a skeletal thing given tendon and muscle by the whorls and twists of plant growth within it. Green stems, fibrous and inky dark in the half light, twisted around the rusting metal struts and curled up towards the night sky. Deep inside the greenhouse itself, lost in the tangle of plants, unrecognisable shapes hung like the stilled hearts of long-dead creatures. The grass around my feet hadn't been cut in years and was creeping in from the scabbed lawn to lie over the concrete flags that formed a path from gate to door. It was up to my knees, twisted around itself and dotted with the bobbing heads of dandelions. Here and there, taller weeds emerged from the mess, raising themselves on leaves that were large and veiny. The lawn whispered to itself as I went along the path, secretive, moving in a breeze I could not feel.

Behind the greenhouse, leaning against the side fence, were old bicycles and what looked like a child's scooter, dirty and rusting. It was impossible to tell exactly how many bikes there were as plants and grass had grown up through the spokes and around the frames and seats, tying each of the machines to the others in a chaos of tubular metal and peeling stickers and corroding rubber. None of the bikes were large.

When I came close enough to the building to see it clearly, I realised that someone had tried to burn it in the past. Along the base of the wall there was a series of misshapen black flowers growing, smears of soot and scorch marks stretching up the brickwork. There was a bundle of partly incinerated twigs and branches against one of the marks, the pale bones of unburned wood showing though the charcoal darkness.

The light was still hovering behind the window, but it was less regular, and I wondered if someone had broken in and was searching the place using a candle for illumination. Even candlelight wouldn't account for the way the light wavered, though, not flickering so much as fading to almost nothing before struggling back up to a pale, anaemic yellow. I tried standing on tiptoe to look through the holes in the sheet covering the window, but it was too high for me to reach, so I had to mount the steps to the door. The metal sheet covering the entrance was, I saw, not as solidly attached to the stonework as it appeared, and it took very little pressure to shift it along, tilting it at the bottom so that a space into the house opened up. A smell emerged, like opening an oven door on fish that has baked too long and yet, underneath, was something else, a smell of marshmallows; my favourite scent, and my mouth watered slightly as it tickled at my nose. The space filled briefly with the waning light, and I peered in, hoping to see something. All I needed was something concrete, I told myself, something I could ring the police about, and I could leave the Merry House and never enter its grounds again. I could go back to my dogs, my Terri, to Dominic and to my life.

There was nothing there.

Without putting my head into the hole, I could see only part of the hallway, a section of the kitchen and a little of the room that opened off the hallway opposite the kitchen. The floors were uncarpeted, the boards bare and un-even, and the far end of the hallway lost to thick shadows. The kitchen was un-furnished, the cupboards lining the walls stained with splashes of something dark, and its stylings were older, dated. From overhead, a wooden clothes airing rail hung down unevenly, the ropes that held it frayed and knotted. Cobwebs hung from the walls and dust lay across the floors, although there were streaks through it that exposed the knotholed wood below. In the cor-ner of the kitchen, I saw another small burned patch: one cupboard door was charred across its bottom edge and warped so that it hung awkwardly, not quite fitting in the frame. In the further room, I could see a sliver of something that looked like an old sofa, brown and mottled with mould. I wondered just how long it was since someone had lived in the bungalow.

There was no light, and no noise. If the building was empty, what had I seen? Water? Water in one of the rooms reflected by the light from the streetlamps? My imagination? With a last look into the house, at the sagging and grimy interior, I stood and made to leave. There was nothing here, I told myself, save darkness and night and I should go home. I began to manhandle the metal sheet back over the doorway, wincing as it cried out, the anguished wail of metal kissing stone, and then realised that under the shriek I could hear singing.

At first I thought it was a distant drunk, but it wasn't; the voice was coming from within the house. I yanked the sheet back from the doorway, dropping to my knees in front of the gap and listening. Whoever was singing, they were crying as they sang, making the words incomprehensible. The glow increased, filling the air with that diseased yellow glimmer. I leaned my head into the hole slightly, hoping to see something, to hear more clearly, and jumped back, startled.

There was a little girl standing in the doorway of the room opposite the kitchen.

The light was coming from somewhere behind her, was surrounding her in a corona of muzzy yellow that distorted her edges, making her seem not quite there. That it was a girl was obvious; silhouette pigtails with bows tied at their ends were visible. She was singing and crying, her voice high and sweet and brittle.

"Hello," I said, keeping my voice calm, "are you okay?" Such a stupid question, so infantile, but what else could I say? What else was there to ask? She didn't respond except for to carry on singing, a song I knew from Dominic and from my own childhood: the wheels on the bus, going round and round and round. You used to sing it to me, making those stupid swishing noises when we did the verse about the wipers, do you remember?

"Sandra?" I asked. "Sandra Cahill? Is that you? Come here, sweetie, and we'll get you home."

At the sound of her name, Sandra took a step forward, moving into the hallway. She was only two or three feet from the back door, from me, but I still couldn't see her properly; the light was swallowing her, distorting her. She was singing on, crying.

"Sandra," I said again. "Come here, and we'll get you back to your mum and dad." I started to squeeze in through the narrow gap, pushing against the edges of the metal sheet with my shoulders, widening the hole as best I could. The smell in the house was terrible, a kind of overheated, baking sourness, the smell of feverish sweat and sex and dampness and old saliva. I reached out a hand to Sandra, the edge of the metal digging into my side and catching on my belt, and said again, "Come here, sweetie, and we'll get you home." She took another step, finally moving out of the grasp of the light that came from behind her, and her face emerged into the pale shadows. I screamed.

Sandra's mouth was almost sealed, strings of peeling skin that looked like parchment stretching between her lips, and her eyes were milky and wide, blind. Something had spilled from her nose and dried to a crusted, cracking black and her hair was matted and limp across her forehead. More blackness spilled from her mouth as she sang, rivulets dribbling around the stretching skin, down her chin and onto her chest and folded arms; it stank, and I realised that the smell in the house was coming, at least in part, from her. She was bathed in the odour, as though she had rolled in loose and watery bowel movements and then let it dry against her skin. "Sandra," I managed to say, reaching out with one hand to her, encouraging her to keep moving. Whatever had happened to her, whoever had done it, we had to get away from this place *now*.

She took another step, stumbled, looked towards me with pallid, dried-milk eyes, and then stopped singing. "It was such a pretty thing, and I just wanted to see it," she whispered, "and now it won't let me go. Why won't it let me go?" Her voice was thick, gluey with barely repressed pain and misery. "I want my mummy," she said and took another step, was almost within reach, and then she jerked violently. I lunged, grasped at her and missed as she jerked again, fell and was dragged backwards across the hallways and through the door. The glow brightened, drew her in, and from behind me I heard my dogs bark frenziedly. I think I may have screamed again then; I'm not sure. Somewhere nearby, as if in descant to the dogs, a cat began to howl.

Sandra cried out, shrieked, and then began singing again, the wheels on the bus still going round and round and round like a mantra set against an awfulness I could only imagine. I thrashed, dragging my belt loose from the metal sheet and pulling myself into the Merry House, scrambling across the floor. The dust felt greasy on my hands, the boards rough under it, and splinters worked their way into my palms and fingers. I pulled out my mobile phone, but there was no signal and I cursed it and tried dialling the police anyway, cursing again when it didn't work. I wanted to stop, to go back and call from outside, but I couldn't. The memory of Sandra's face, of the black liquid spattering from her mouth amid the stink of corruption, and the miserable singing from somewhere in the house drew me on.

Where the yellow light fell against my skin, it burned, as though I had been exposed for too long to sunlight that was stained and dirty. Its source was not in the first room, which contained just the old sofa, but in the room beyond, through a second doorway in the far wall. I moved towards it, trying to shield my face and skin against the light, hating the way it felt against me and the way my eyes watered despite its apparent weakness. Something dark moved in the heart of the light, thrashing against that weak glare, writhing. Sandra made a choking sound and said, "Mummy," and then fell silent, and I could do nothing but run to her, crying her name.

The next room wasn't a room at all, but something else. I can't explain what, exactly, but it was vast, cavernous, glowing and raging with flames and the stink of loss. The space dropped away from the doorway, falling an impossible distance from me and rising an impossible distance above me. It wasn't an open space, however, but was divided, honeycombed by what looked like torn and hanging curtains of flesh, muscles and fat bunching and clenching and making the room contract and loosen around me.

Here and there, dangling from those shifting, weeping walls were cables that looked like writhing ganglia, and at the end of them were the husks of children. They were crumpled, their hair strawlike and lank, their skin roughened and dry, their limbs withered and white, and there were seemingly hundreds, thousands, more than I could count. Some still moved, twisting and thrashing weakly, their hands held out in front of them, shivering or punching at the air. Sounds filled the place, airless, hollow moans, weeping, and occasional cries. All the children were naked.

Sandra was held in the air above me.

She was caught, I saw, by one of those black, weaving tendrils that snaked up from the place below. It pulsed and moved as it held her, bucking her back and forth, shaking her in a savage palsy. Something was being drawn out of her; I could see it, surging back along that black tube, making it bulge rhythmically. Even as I watched, Sandra's arms seemed to shrivel, her legs to pull up like drying paper, her skin to wrinkle and peel. Her shoes fell from her feet as they curled up, and another one of the tendrils tore her dress away, leaving her clad only in socks and white panties, before punching into the skin of her chest. The pants had the word *Tuesday* and a picture of a princess printed on the front, and when I saw that I sobbed. In a voice that was weak and dustlike, Sandra said, "It was so pretty, and I only wanted to see it and hold it. I'm sorry, Mummy, I didn't mean to be naughty. I'll be good, I promise. I promise." She began singing again as her belly folded in on itself, gasping and jerking even as the wheels went around and around and around and as her moistness and life were finally sucked out. More of the tendrils rose up and pierced into her, tearing away first her socks and then her pants, Tuesday's princess fluttering down into the fleshy catacombs below.

When she was little more than a folded, crumpled caricature of the neat blond girl who had greeted Dominic and me occasionally in the playground in the mornings, the tendrils relaxed, and Sandra dropped away to join the other dangling, desiccated corpses.

Another tendril rose in front of me, this one without a child at its end; instead, it held a shifting, blackly glinting mass that smelled of marshmallows and Terri after a shower and Dominic in the morning when he had just woken up; it smelled of comfort and safety and excitement and pleasure. In the centre of the mass I saw a swirling mess of all the fabulous things I had seen in my life; here was my wife, naked on a bed on our wedding night, there Dominic asleep, here the curve of my first girlfriend's neck, there the sun reflecting on water that I just knew was warm and inviting, and I felt myself take a step towards it. It darted closer to me, snakelike, now shaping itself into an image of our first dog when she was a puppy and smelling like newly baked biscuits, and now back to my wife, dressed this time but smiling at me and loving me, to Dominic holding out his arms for a hug, so trusting, and then I remembered Sandra collapsing in on herself and I saw the jagged teeth that chattered at the edge of the mass, and I turned and ran.

I didn't tell anyone. How could I? What could I say? That I had seen Sandra, seen the thing that had fished her out of Scale Hall with a lure made of... what? All the things she loved? Everything she wanted to see and hold and experience again? What would it be for her, I wondered? Teddies or dolls, Christmas presents, her parents? What else could I say? That the fishing thing had been doing it for years, had fished all those lost children from this place, all of them vanished and gone, sucked dry and left to dangle like insects caught on flypaper? No. People would think me mad.

I remember little about my dash home except that when I got out of the Merry House, clambering through the hole in the doorway and then pushing at the gate, the dogs wouldn't let me near them. Although I managed to unclip the leads from the college fence, they strained to escape from me all the way home, their hackles high and their lips drawn back from teeth that were only slightly whiter than the gums in which they sat. It took them days to be comfortable with me, because I *smelled*; I could almost taste the stench of that place on myself, smell it on my skin and in my sweat. I ended burning all the clothes I had been wearing because, even after washing, they were sour with its smell. I haven't walked past the Merry House since then, have stayed as far from it as I can, and it has sat in my nightmares each night.

It has followed me, and has set its lure towards Dominic. I have no idea if it is a deliberate thing, an attempt to silence me, or simply the blind appetite of a thing I cannot hope to understand and that has smelled or tasted my son somehow, but I know that he is being hooked by it. Even as I write this, he is watching something that I cannot see, standing at the garden gate and looking along the road in the direction of the Merry House. If I tell him to stop, I know that it will take me several attempts to gain his attention, and that even if he does come away from the gate, it won't be long before he is back there. How long before he waits until my back is turned and tries to go to it? How long? Minutes? Hours? How long can I keep my eyes on him? How long before my son becomes one of the dry, crumpled things hanging from clawing, sucking tubes that have drained the vitality out of him?

How long?

I keep thinking about fire, about the lichen patterns of soot and burning on the outside of the Merry House, about the patch inside. About other adults, perhaps, who saw something of the things that I saw and tried to take action. Perhaps the fire needs to be deeper, though, set into the heart of the fishing thing so that it cannot escape the flames. Whatever it is, however it has managed to break through the skin between worlds, it is sending out its lines and catching things, catching *children*, and it needs stopping. It should beware; sometimes, those who fish may catch sharks.

I shall go to it tonight, carrying matches and fluid that flames easily. I do not have the luxury of hoping I will return, but what choice do I have? I love Terri and love the life we have made, and don't want to lose it, but I love Dominic, and cannot risk him coming to harm. I cannot let him be *fished*. If I am to be the sacrifice that allows them to live on, then so be it. What else can I do? What? I love you, Dad, and Mum as well.

Pray for me; pray for Dominic.

Pray for Scale Hall.

Nakata 3: University Office

"There's a place you need to know about," said the voice into Nakata's ear. It was heavy, masculine, wary, and as he listened to the rest of the message, he decided that it was probably another hoax. He'd had so many of them over the previous weeks, so many more were coming in every day because of the all the places that Tidyman had paid to have the advert placed, that most of his days were spent simply listening, noting and deleting. The majority of calls remained well-meaning but useless, *my dad said, my brother told me, I heard about,* unverifiable, anonymous, the outpourings of people who believed, and mistook their surety for proof. Then came the jokes, the hoaxes, the insults, and trailing a long way behind, the calls that might bear further investigation.

Nakata's finger was over the button to delete the message when he stopped. The voice had continued, slow and inexorable. "It's a place where things have happened, where people say that they've seen things and had things done to them. You can check it out, it's well known in the area even though people don't like talking about it." It wasn't what the person was saying, exactly, that stopped him; rather, it was the tone of voice, studied and serious but with a waver of nervous honesty. *Either this person's a liar and a great actor*, he thought, *or they at least believe what they're saying.* The problem was, most of the people who left messages *believed*; what they didn't have was proof. It was all faith, faith and trust and hope, nothing that Nakata could use. He listened to the rest of the message, went to delete it, and then stopped again. It was anonymous, and he had set himself the rule that he wouldn't attempt to follow up anonymous tips, but still. . . but still. This had, he was irritated to admit, got to him. He listened to the message again, jotting the details down in his notebook, and then booted up his computer. As the guts of the machine whirred and grouched to themselves, he listened to the message a third time, trying to work out what it was about the words or the voice that had convinced him. He still couldn't tell.

The internet, when his computer had woken fully, gave him more details, although not many. There were several newspaper articles about the place, which he downloaded and saved, scanning each briefly. Two were short, the third (with the title 'What Haunts This Place?') longer but more hysterical. They were no help. He also found references to the place on a number of websites, most of which dealt with it solely as an area of outstanding beauty or historical interest. The last one he went to, however, listed what it called 'a comprehensive overview of the incidents recorded', setting out dates and including references. Nakata printed the page off, now intrigued. If there were references, then he had at least the start of trail. Taking his map from the shelf, he discovered that the place wasn't that far away. Turning back to the internet, he read more.

What clinched it for him, finally, was finding a blog written by someone calling himself LocalBoy, which recounted two separate incidents that the author claimed to have had at the place. *It shouldn't be hard to contact them,* Nakata thought, *and see if they'll go on record. That's enough to start with, anyway.* He turned back to his notes, already planning in his head when he could go. He opened the street map to the right page and compared it with what the anonymous messenger had told him. "Go beyond the graves, and wait.

"Go beyond the graves, and they will come to you."

Beyond St Patrick's Chapel, Heysham Head

Nakata stood in the sunlight, letting it warm his face. The taxi's engine receded to a low growl like a distant dog before fading away entirely, and he was able to properly take stock. Tilting his head back and closing his eyes, he caught the warmth in his mouth like falling raindrops. He felt as though the weight of something had been lifted from him, although what, he couldn't precisely say. He was glad to be out of the oppressively heavy atmosphere of his office and its small but growing stack of files for Tidyman, certainly, and to get out into the open again; it felt like months since he had breathed air that wasn't hemmed in by brick and claustrophobia. *I should have brought a picnic with me*, he thought, *and turned this into a proper adventure*. It didn't matter that this was still part of his work for Tidyman, that he expected it to turn out to be nothing. It was an excuse, a rare excuse, nothing more, a chance to get away for a few hours and to charge his time to someone else, and he was determined to enjoy it. Eventually, when his lungs felt empty of the pressures of typing and endless voicemail messages and certainty without proof, with Tidyman's odd commission fading like the taxi's noise, he opened his eyes.

The village of Heysham appeared small, three or four shops and a restaurant in a cluster around a space that felt like it should be a village green but was in fact a car park whose flat grey apron was covered in the segregations of paint and oil stains, the bays like tattoos faded and dull under old skin. There was a burnt-out takeaway sitting on one edge of the car park, its roof missing and its walls inked with old flame and soot and rain. There was almost no sound, and Nakata could see no one. He checked the map in his pocket, and turned.

It shouldn't be far, so he started walking. The road dropped, curving alongside a pub, more shops, and a small, closed tourist information office. Strolling, he left them behind and passed a garden that contained beehives, but he did not stop to look at them; he had never liked bees. As he walked, he thought again about what he was here for. This was not a trip about answers; he was sure that there were none here, despite the message on his voicemail. This was about space, he thought, space and faith. After all the insistency contained in the voicemail messages, after all the false leads and dead ends and uncertainty, his trip to Heysham was about nothing more than renewal. His own, and maybe that of his faith.

St Peter's Church was at the end of the road, as his map said it would be. It was tiny, the stone wall surrounding it enclosing a picture-postcard graveyard, a mix of new gravestones and older, tumbled markers. Although he couldn't see the far sides, he knew that the graveyard went all around the church, and that at the far side were graves right up to the edge of the cliffs. The air was tangy with salt, and the sea was a pale blue strip behind the church. He wondered how he had lived in the area so long and had never visited before, how he had become so insular and closed off. Amy would never have allowed him to get like this.

Nakata didn't enter the church grounds; instead, he carried on alongside its wall and up the old steps that led to the ruins of St Patrick's Chapel. There wasn't much left, merely some groundworks and foundations that revealed themselves in level changes in the earth, and segments of thick walls. Around the remains of the ancient building, the ground was flat and grassed.

Nearby were six short hollows carved into the earth.

They looked like graves, and were just as the unknown messenger had described them; all in a row and carved into the rock itself, their shapes vaguely suggestive of shrouded corpses. None was longer than five feet, and all six were dank with rainwater that had nowhere to soak away to and with litter caught in the water's embrace, sun-bleached and sodden. Moss climbed along the stone lip of several of the hollows, which were perhaps two feet deep, although it was hard to judge the depth accurately because the lightless water that gathered in them.

A sepia information board set like an insubstantial wall along the edge of one of the boundary lines of the old chapel told Nakata that the hollows were probably Viking graves dating from the eleventh or twelfth century, that they might have once contained two or more bodies each or been used multiple times as the corpses in them mouldered and decayed, but they might have been something else entirely, that no one was sure. *Faith and uncertainty*, thought Nakata briefly, *it's all there is.*

From St Patrick's Chapel, there was only one way to go; left, along Heysham Head, the name for the coastal cliff that stretched between the village and the next beach, Half Moon Bay. The land itself was steeply sloped, rising from the cliff edge to a higher plateau, and from the chapel there were two worn paths Nakata could take. One went high, following the wall that ran along the top of the Head, separating the public ground from the houses beyond, and the lower one followed the cliff edge. *Take the lower*, the unknown caller had said, *it's not far from the graves that things happen.* With a last look around, Nakata set off.

He moved slowly at first, enjoying the openness and the view. The sea was on his right, another fifty or so feet below him, its surface like battered glass. The distant solidity of Barrow's headlands were visible across the water, made clean and fresh by the sunlight and the scents in the air. Long grass swayed around his feet, leaving wet streaks across the toecaps of his boots and loosening the mud that was caked into the grips and ridges of his soles so that it dropped behind him as he walked, tiny pieces of shadow left on the surface of the grass. Dandelions waved languorously in the late morning breeze, their puffball heads bobbing white against the greenery. Buttercups and daisies were dotted about like freckles of colour on the skin of the earth, and patches of darker green bracken crawled the slope above him. After a few minutes' walk, the lower path moved away from the cliff edge, the ground ahead of him smoothing and flattening so that it was like walking across a field that had been sheared off at his side. The air was warm and he could hear birds singing in the distance.

After another few minutes walking, during which both the cliff and the path carried on curving around, Nakata found himself in a natural depression, enclosed by earth, air and water. It looked like a small amphitheatre scooped out of the earth, its boundaries formed by the cliff on one side and the rising slope on the other. The worn path carried on across its middle before the slope and the cliff met again several hundred yards away and carried on together around the head. Nakata heard nothing but the distant grumble of the sea against the rocks and the seabirds' crying. It was peaceful here, he thought, calm and unhurried and pleasant. Close to the cliff edge, which showed as a black line against the bracken and grass, the remains of a fence had emerged from the tangled plants, the wooden posts bent at angles like rotten teeth. Rusted wire lay in coils around the posts and beyond them the sea's surface undulated with a movement like a snake's locomotion.

Ridges in the rising amphitheatre wall made convenient seats, and Nakata clambered up several of them before sitting, the tails of his coat protecting him from the wet; since his time with Wisher in the café, he avoided being damp. From his newly elevated position, he had a good view of the journey he had taken. He had come off the established path, he saw, bent and broken grass marking his passage across the flat ground, a shambling and irregular wander that jagged towards the cliff and away again, juddering across the field in one direction and then another. He had not realised that he had walked in such a ragged way, lost to the enjoyment of his senses. He was surprised to realise just how far he had walked along the Head, at least half a mile, perhaps a little more. Because of the angle of the slope and the way the Head was formed, both the chapel and the church beyond it were lost to view and all he could see was the grassy slopes about him and the water beyond. This was the place.

In the bowl, the caller had said, and it did look like a bowl, open above and to the front. Nakata looked around, but there was nothing unusual to see or hear. He let out a sigh that loosed even more tension from his flesh, and grinned broadly. *I'm in the bowl*, he thought. *There are worse places to be.* He let out another refreshing breath. This was *fun*.

When Nakata looked at his watch, he was astonished to find that it was lunchtime. His stomach rumbled, reminding him that it was hours since he had eaten, and he decided to return to Heysham and get some food. There was nothing here for him, although perhaps the morning might not be wasted if someone in the village could be persuaded to go on record about this place. He made to rise, and stopped.

There were tracks across the grass.

Rather, there was a second trail made by a person walking through the grass, marked out by the shadows created by the sun catching against the pooled and broken stems of grass. It emerged from the foliage at the cliff edge, level with where his own tracks moved away from the path and closed in until it was perhaps twenty or twenty five yards distant from the marks of his passage, running parallel to them before stopping abruptly a hundred yards away from where he was seated. Nakata scanned the rest of the ground carefully, but could see no other signs that people had been there recently. The rest of the grass was unbroken, swaying in an almost unfelt breeze. He looked back at the other trail.

Its end seemed closer to him.

There was nowhere for someone to hide if they were following him, so it couldn't have been extended whilst he looked around; there was no one else here to extend it. As he peered about, he caught sight of the start of another trail that had not, he was sure, been there a moment ago. It was only short, maybe twenty feet or so, but it was clear, emerging onto the grass a little closer to his current position than the first track did. He looked about; there were definitely no other trails. He looked back at his own markings, which were unchanged. The first track, however, now finished closer to him, only fifty yards away.

Nakata took a deep breath, wondering. An animal? No. He looked down at his feet. The grass was curled, reaching up to almost cover his feet, but that still meant it was only four or five inches high; there was not the cover to hide a creature big enough to make the trails. He looked back to find that the nearest had leapt ten yards closer and the further one had stretched itself out to almost double its original length. Two more trials had started to crawl out from the grass by the cliff, both short but clearly outlined. Nothing in the field moved besides the waving stems, making the trails shimmer slightly. Nakata blinked deliberately and slowly. When he opened his eyes, all four trails had come closer. A further new one now emerged from up the slope, above the path.

As a child, Nakata had gone out with fishermen and had thought that there must be some magic to the way in which they knew where to go to find the greatest hauls. Later, he realised that they were taking in and analysing all sorts of tiny pieces of the world and were reading its textures and breath accurately and to their profit. The weather, the look of the sea, the temperature, the light, the time of year; all of them interacted to give these water- and air-beaten men the location of the fish. As an adult, he tried hard to make the decisions that ruled his life the same way, based on everything he could see and hear and feel and prove, despite recognising in himself a certain need for the world to be bigger, more expansive than his senses told him it was. It was why he was a good researcher and academic, because he refused to simply *believe*, he would always try to *prove*. He had a faith, surely, but it was one tempered by a cynic's need for more than simply hopeful belief. It was part of the reason that Tidyman wanted him, he assumed, that and what had happened at the Glasshouse Estate, because he would prod and poke at a thing until he had an explanation, even if that explanation was one neither he nor anyone else wanted or expected. Now, sitting with his back to the slope and the curious trails ahead of him, he thought, *There is no reason to fear these trails.* Whatever was making them could not be large. Despite what the anonymous message had said, there surely could be no threat here; these were only markings in wet grass.

In the moments that he had thought this, the trails had come slightly closer to him. The nearest one was now only thirty feet away.

Nakata rose and stepped back down on to his own trail carefully, turning slightly sideways as he did so to give himself the best balance possible and to keep the closest of the new trails in view. In three long steps, he was away from the amphitheatre wall and out into the flatter ground at the bottom of the bowl. He surveyed the ground ahead of him. The trails were much harder to see from this lower elevation and he had completely lost sight of the further ones; the nearer one was a smudged shadow against the grass, appearing and disappearing as he walked like one of those illusory pictures, first a jumble of meaningless lines, then a coherent shape, and then back again. He moved slowly back along his own trail, placing his feet within the lines drawn by his previous passage, retracing his steps as accurately as he could. He was soon alongside the end of the nearest trail and then past it. He moved another few steps forward and then turned.

The trail, now behind him, had twisted and was following him. It reminded him unpleasantly of a worm burrowing through the dirt just below the surface of the earth, its blunt head questing ceaselessly onwards.

Turning his back on it again, he walked on. His path took him close to the cliff edge again and the ragged, decrepit fences with their aging wire loomed into view, torn plastic bags flapping in trapped helplessness on the rusting metal loops. Here he pivoted, intending to follow his earlier route away from the cliff and back towards the church. Shocked, however, he remained motionless.

There were now six trails converging on him.

The closest was still the one that he had first seen and which had followed him across the field and was now within ten feet of him. He saw flattened grass and crushed daisies, their white heads twisted and flattened, in the path's centre; looking at his own tracks, he saw exactly the same patterns of destruction. The other trails were further away but were approaching from all sides. None of them moved in straight lines, he noticed. They angled one way and then another, but their focus was clear. They were coming for *him*. Suddenly unnerved, he stepped away from the cliff, but doing so brought him closer to the trails. Even in the action of stepping forwards, when he had briefly flicked his eyes to the ground and then looked up again, they had advanced. If they were being made by people he could have reached out and touched the nearest one, gripped them by the arm and asked them what they were doing.

There was no one there.

Nakata stepped towards a gap in the trails, moving more quickly than he had intended but experiencing a fear that was as formless and deep as the ones that he remembered from that last night in the house on the Glasshouse Estate. It was suddenly important to put distance between the trails and him, yet he refused to allow himself to panic. *Stay rational,* he demanded of himself. Whatever the trails were, whatever was creating them, no matter how strongly his instincts were telling him that to let these strange trails catch him would not merely be bad, it would be fucking terrible, he had to stay *rational*. Panic would lead to mistakes, and he had the clear, terrifying sense that mistakes now might prove fatal.

As Nakata passed the closest trail, a cold breeze grasped at him, finding the gaps in his clothes and licking at his skin. He jerked away from the clammy, sickly breeze, stumbling and falling to his knees. The damp soaked through his trousers and chilled his flesh, and where it touched him the moisture felt as slimy and oily as the breeze had done. He scrambled forwards, knowing that the trails were about to catch him, were about to be upon him. He pulled himself to his feet and, spinning on one heel, jumped. The trails had turned again, he saw, were closer still, stalking him.

His leap took Nakata into open space, the nearest of the trails a slightly more comfortable distance away. Curiously, he lifted his foot; the ground under it was ripped and muddy where he had landed and pivoted, a small scar cutting through the grass and showing the darker earth underneath. Similar patterns of damage decorated the nearest trails, tiny punctuation marks that indicated where they had already jagged about, changing direction to follow him. Something had pivoted, turned around to chase him as he passed. He kept his eyes on the nearest trails, reasoning that if they only moved when he was not looking, then he would keep them in view.

Nakata realised almost immediately, however, that this was impossible. He could look at the two or three closest to him, but not the ones at the periphery of his vision or that were further back, and they moved as he concentrated on their companions. In the last few brief moments, two of the trails had moved around him and were trying to get behind him. Alarmed, feeling as though he were being stalked and herded simultaneously, he pushed further away from the path and into the deserted centre of the grass, wondering what he should do. It wasn't a hard decision.

Nakata ran.

He turned and leapt over the nearest trail, feeling that breeze again, unhealthy and clinging, and then he landed and accelerated into a run. His legs pistoned, and the air was cold in his lungs as he ran. The earth conspired against him, ridges and humps in the ground threatening to trip him, tiny gulleys catching his boots and sharp stones rolling under his soles, unbalancing him. He did not dare risk glancing back over his shoulder as he ran, focusing only on keeping ahead of the trails. He imagined a hollow, low whistle as they followed him, a fierce whipping as the grass was beaten and flattened, torn aside by flesh as solid as it was invisible. The rattle of his breath and the soft squelching of his feet smacking the ground capered loudly in his ears. Ahead of him the ground was criss-crossed with the trails, and he knew-felt inside-that he had to avoid treading on them; his instincts for self-preservation told him so. Rationality be damned now; rationality had no place in this, there was only flight and faith, the faith that he was in a danger that went further than the merely physical.

Coming to the first of the trails he jumped, landing heavily on the far side and almost losing his balance. He took several clumsy steps and then jumped again, clearing a further trail in a headlong stagger. His arms kept a rhythm, providing him with balance, flashing in counterpoint to his legs. He zigzagged, running parallel to one trail and then another. Somehow, they seemed to be circling around him, closing in, despite his never seeing them move. His face grew hot as he ran, the sweat gathering under his arms and down the centre of his back, and then he was jumping again, the trails vanishing beneath him only to reappear ahead of him, jerking and irregular.

He was coming around the Head now, leaving the amphitheatre behind but the trails were coming with him, pacing him and there was another noise now, a roar of things that might have been beasts or men; it was impossible to tell. The slope, now on his right, was coming closer, bunching him and the trails together in the narrowing gap between it and the cliff. Bracken whipped at his legs, and still the ground tried to trip him. The trails, moving with the nightmare jitter of bad stop-motion animations, were closing in and he thought that this was it, that everything so far had been leading to this point.

The raised plateau of St Patrick's Chapel appeared ahead of him and Nakata put on a burst of flailing speed, leaping again as one of the trails, the original one he knew without knowing how he knew, darted at his feet. He landed hard, the shock dancing up his legs and stuttering his rhythm, and for a ragged, endless moment he thought he was going to fall and that all would be done and over, and then he somehow found his centre of gravity and pulled it back. Another leap, and then he was at the plateau and jumping clumsily up onto it, not stopping running. The graves flashed past on his left and then the trails were once again about him, merging and splitting, splitting and merging and then he was at the far edge and was dropping to the road that ran down by St Peter's Church.

The road was metalled, muddy and leaf-strewn but solid beneath him, and he let himself stop running. His legs trembled violently, sweat drizzled into his eyes and his breath was torn and sharp in his throat. He dropped to his knees, ignoring the mud and dirt, breathing as deeply as he could, feeling a vicious stitch start and then fade in his side and thinking, oddly, how unfit he was; another thing he had let slip since Amy and the Glasshouse Estate.

Finally, Nakata had the strength to rise, despite legs that still felt weak and kittenish. Overcoming his fear, he went close to the steps leading up to the raised ground and chapel beyond, and looked carefully across the grass. There were no trails to be seen. Shadows stretched from dents and punctures in the uneven ground, but these were irregular, detached from each other.

Normal.

He climbed the steps, being careful not to let his feet leave the old stone and stray onto the grass. The plateau was unmarked except for one trail, his own. Confused and disturbed, he scrubbed at his face with his wet, dirty hands. Distantly, he heard the sound of seagulls. A car horn blared; another replied. What had happened here? He didn't know, couldn't guess. He felt empty and bitter, full of sour adrenaline and fear. What had happened here? *What?*

The chapel looked on, impassive, as the smell of sweet grass and dark earth filled Nakata's nostrils.

Nakata 4: Meeting Room 1

"Wait here," said the attendant, and left the room. Nakata looked about him; the room wasn't what he expected. He had imagined it would be plain, austere, designed to intimidate and dampen the emotions of the people within it, but it wasn't; instead of the plain table and uncomfortable chairs he expected, there were three easy chairs, a television on a small stand and a table holding a plastic vase, flowers and a box of tissues. Thick carpet covered the floor and there were two pictures on the walls, prints of innocuous watercolours. One was a seascape; the beach in the foreground reminded Nakata of Heysham Head. He shivered, involuntary, and focused back in on the room.

There were no windows, no natural daylight, but the walls were painted a muted yellow that was warm and cheery. The only signs that this wasn't a normal room were the small CCTV camera in the upper corner and the fact that the door locked automatically behind the attendant after he left.

Nakata flicked open his notebook to read his notes again, not to remind him of anything but because he was nervous. Arranging this meeting had taken several weeks, time that Tidyman told him repeatedly that he did not have, and he had no guarantee that it would prove to be of use. There was simply that faith again, a hunch based on talking to the man's daughter and on reading the documents she had already sent him. Most of them were in his bag, although he had been asked to leave the bag itself in the office as he wasn't allowed to bring it to the meeting. *Paper and a pencil only*, he had been told. *Make notes or remember*.

Meeting Room 1 was just inside the two sets of double doors that acted like an airlock: on entering, the first set had been locked behind him before the second set was opened. Before he had been escorted into the room, Nakata had heard the sound of a distant television. He heard no human voices, no screams, no moans or gibbering. He was relieved, and irritated at his relief; those sounds only populated places like this in bad films, he was sure. *I'll be wanting to see an insane old woman next, with long hair and grimy clothes*, he said to himself, rueful and amused in equal measure. *Amy'll laugh when I tell her*, he thought before remembering that Amy wouldn't laugh at this or anything else.

The door behind Nakata opened and the attendant re-entered the room, escorting an older man who looked at Nakata warily and then sat in the chair opposite him. He limped badly as he walked, and winced as he sat. There were a series of scars wrapped around his exposed forearm, lithe and twisting, visible because he was dressed in jeans and a plain T-shirt. When he stretched out his legs in front of him, wincing again, his jeans pulled back to reveal thin, hairless ankles that had more scars written upon their pale skin. The man looked to be in his seventies, possibly older. Nakata knew he was only just fifty. The attendant remained standing by the door.

"My daughter said to talk to you," the man said without preamble. "What do you want to know?"

"The truth of it. Of what you saw, heard, what your friends said they heard, saw. . Everything. I want to know what happened," replied Nakata. "I've read what you were accused of. . ."

"Found guilty of," said the man, interrupting.

"Yes," said Nakata. "Found guilty of. I've read the court transcripts, seen some of the documentation, the things your daughter has copies of, and I wanted to know the full story. Your defence was an unusual one, hard to believe. It seems a strange defence to use."

"It was the truth," said the man, his voice weary. "I believe in the truth. Don't you?"

"Yes," said Nakata, "I do. Do you still believe it? The things you said in court? That they happened?"

"Yes. Why?"

"I'm collecting stories like yours," said Nakata, "for a project I'm involved in. I can't tell you any more than that, I'm afraid, other than it's nothing sensationalistic. If the project is successful, it may help someone. Someone in a position like yours."

"How can I help anyone?" asked the man. "I'm mad, haven't you heard? Insane." He sounded bitter, bowing his head as he spoke. An ugly twist of scar tissue curled up across his scalp, visible through his thinning grey hair as a pale pink tangled worm.

"You don't seem insane," said Nakata.

"No? And you'd know?"

"I have some experience of situations like the ones you described."

"I doubt that," the man said, anger spiking his voice. "I seriously doubt that. And why should you be any different? I told the truth and look where it got me." He raised a hand above his head, shaking a fist. Nakata felt, rather than saw, the attendant take a step away from the door towards the man and raised his own hand.

"There's a good chance I'll believe you," he said to the man quietly. "Please, trust me. I don't believe you're mad."

"Then why did I kill my two friends?" asked the man, his voice low.

"That," said Nakata, "is exactly what I'm hoping you'll tell me."

The Ocean Grand, North West Coast

Arrival; initial impressions.

Mandeville twisted on the key, hard, and felt it grate in the lock. With a final yank, it came around and then the *Ocean Grand* was open for the first time in fifteen years.

The central door was large and heavy and, even unlocked, it took him several hard shoves to open it fully; it had swollen from the years of disuse, clinging and screeching as it moved, cutting tracks through the dirt on the floor. Pieces of crumpled paper shifted away in the light breeze that entered the hotel around Mandeville. Of course, he thought, it wasn't really the first time the building had been open for fifteen years, and he had to be careful not to romanticise the experience or what he found inside. Safety assessors had been inside only recently and security checks were carried out monthly, but he was the first *outsider* to gain entrance since it had closed as a working building in the early nineties. Actually, even that wasn't quite true; a local television news team had accompanied one of the early safety crews and had filmed them placing boards over the wall murals and picture windows. Mandeville had a copy of the footage in his bag. In it, the unseen presenter talked about the glories and controversies of the art deco pieces that adorned the Grand's walls whilst workmen nailed large boards over each piece 'to protect it for the few months that the hotel was shut during its refit'. The 'few months' had turned into almost two hundred, the refit had never occurred. The *Grand* had remained shut to everyone as it changed owners time and again in the intervening years. Until now.

Behind Mandeville, Parry began to unload the van, dropping their gear onto the cracked surface of the car park and telling a joke to Yeoman, the third member of the self-dubbed *Save Our Shit Crew*. Mandeville could already smell the sharp tang of Yeoman's cigarette, and he smiled to himself. Yeoman had said little on the journey, but his silence had become more pointed as they travelled and Parry refused to pull over for a rest stop, claiming that he was helping to break Yeoman's habit by forcing him into periods of abstinence. Yeoman wouldn't enter the *Grand* until he had smoked at least three cigarettes outside, Mandeville knew. It was an old routine, practiced and refined over the previous years until they were all comfortable with it. Leaving them, Mandeville stepped forward into the *Ocean Grand*.

The foyer was large and circular, with the wings branching off through large, arched entrances at his left and right. Opposite Mandeville, the reception desk hugged the curved rear wall, its surface thick with dust. The great staircase rolled around from Mandeville's right, clinging to the wall as it rose before letting onto the floors above the reception. He could just see the dark smears of the doorways leading to the upper bar and the outdoor sun deck. Under his feet, the original wooden flooring was hidden under heavy linoleum, assuming it still existed at all. The light reaching him was dirty and dank; two storeys above him, the atrium's great glass roof was mostly intact but had been covered from the outside with wooden sheets. Where these had peeled back or broken, allowing the light to enter, he saw a film of dirt and old leaves covering the glass. Clicking on his torch, he let the beam play across the roof's frame. It looked to be in fairly good condition, all things considered. There were rust patches, not unexpected given the *Grand's* coastal location, and several of the more delicate sections of the pattern looked to be twisted out of shape. Some of the glass had been removed by the safety team; other panes, he knew, had fallen in long ago, the coloured glass swept up and discarded.

"Can we come in yet?"

"No," said Mandeville. He wanted to savour this; he felt like a time traveller, stepping back into a past placed in storage and only now being brought back to use. The *Ocean Grand* had been decaying for years, not just for the fifteen it had been closed and its ownership a fluid thing; even when it had been open, the rising costs of maintaining a building that had so many unique features had led to a legacy of mismanagement, cost-cutting and barely done repairs, of unique fixtures and fittings falling into disuse, of damage, of art lost and stolen and sold. The hotel was a part of England's industrial and cultural heritage, abused and battered and only now receiving the attention it deserved. Mandeville and his small team, 'Mandeville Art Restoration Projects' officially but who referred to themselves privately as the *Save Our Shit Crew*, had to find out how bad things were in the *Grand*, catalogue what remained and work out what could be saved and what was gone.

Even in the foyer, Mandeville could see evidence of the neglect. There should have been ten balustrade tops in the 'primitive figures' style, cast in metal and spaced every five feet up the staircase, but three were missing. Sections of the reception desk's ornate wooden panelling had been replaced with plain wood sheets, and worst of all, the large panels of the Gravette mural that should have faced the guests as they approached the reception desk were gone. Mandeville knew two were in storage in London; the other two were missing, presumably destroyed or taken when the mural was removed in the early eighties rather than pay for its professional renovation. There was always someone prepared to buy an original Gravette, even one that was painted on a twenty foot by six foot wooden panel and which was only actually a quarter of the whole piece.

To the left of the reception desk was the entrance to the restaurant and, beyond it, the sun corridor. Moving to the doorway, Mandeville saw immediately that sections of the intricate floor designed by Constance Priest were gone. Created by using nearly four thousand handmade tiles, its pattern should have covered the floor, an interlocking swirl of lines and blooms suggesting water, air and life. However, some of the tiles had been replaced by ones that only almost matched and whose colours, size or patterning was just off kilter; other tiles been replaced by plain squares, which cut into Priest's patterns clumsily, disrupting its movement. Mandeville sighed to see it. Tables, cheap Formica models with spindle legs, were piled against the walls like the skeletons of long-dead animals. In the sunlight, the floor pattern and the shadows from the tables merged at the corners of the room, bleeding together in black clots.

The doors to the sun corridor were open, and through them Mandeville could see the grey ocean churning beyond its glass walls. He walked towards it, his feet crunching on the grit and dirt on the floor, and peered into the glass corridor. A later addition to the *Grand* running the length of its rear, the 1950s structure had suffered badly from neglect during the previous years. Streaks of rust crawled down the glass from metal struts that were losing an uneven battle against the corroding, salt-laden atmosphere. Several of the panes were broken and had been replaced by plywood sheets. More sheets lay piled against the seaward wall, having been removed from the windows at Mandeville's request. Apart from the roof in the foyer, all the windows that had complete glass panes had been uncovered so that the crew could work in daylight where possible.

Mandeville was about to leave the sun lounge when he noticed something beyond the glass. No, not beyond the glass, on it: swirls of colour, so incredibly pale as to be almost invisible, but present nonetheless. An arc of red and green straddled the pane nearest to him, blue and red in the next pane along. Stepping close, he ran his fingers across the glass, leaving streaks along the surface. Looking at his fingertips, he saw that the ovals of grime below his nails also contained tiny flashes of colour. Paint? he wondered, sniffing at it. Had someone sprayed or splashed paint on the windows in the past and then tried to wipe it off? Vandalism? He would check with Parry, see if there was a record of that kind of damage; God alone knew what other problems they would come across in here. Turning, he called for his colleagues.

Setting Up; Working the Hotel; Cataloguing

Parry, the crew's archivist and researcher, had set up in the foyer. Laid out across the floor were photocopies and typed sheets, indicating precisely what the crew was to look for and where within the *Grand* it was, how it was made and the materials used. Where makers were known, this was indicated as well. Yeoman, the architect, who had less to do in this initial phase, was setting up a base camp in the restaurant. The crew was staying in the hotel, sleeping in the open expanse of the empty dining area to save time. There was a lot to do, and they had only a week to do it before the owners wanted an initial report. In seven days, Mandeville had to be able to make initial recommendations about the order of jobs and which parts of the hotel's original decorations could be preserved or restored and incorporated into the latest developments planned for the hotel. It was a big job, the biggest the crew had taken on.

Mandeville was rereading the initial site assessment carried out by the owner's own assessors. There were a couple of areas in the hotel the crew had been instructed to stay away from (the kitchen; not an issue as there was nothing in there for them to assess according to Parry, and a first floor bathroom whose floor was rotten but which Mandeville did want to check out if he could). Up or down? he asked himself. Top or bottom first? Finally, he chose bottom simply because the closest of what Parry called his 'Interest Lists' dealt with ground floor. Taking the sheet of paper, Mandeville moved into one of the *Grand's* lower corridors.

Parry was in the top corridor. Unlike Mandeville, the artist and restorer, or Yeoman, the architect, Parry was a historian and he simply wanted to see what remained of the hotel's past. Of course, the great delight in being part of the *Save Our Shit Crew* was that sometimes they could persuade those designers of the present and the future to save or incorporate the past into their plans. Take this place, for example; the *Ocean Grand*. Originally owned by one of Britain's smaller rail companies, the *Grand* was the crowning glory of the artists Howard Gravette and Marie Priest, and the only hotel they had ever designed. Working with the architect, Edward Manning, they had created a small, opulent establishment, intended for the monied classes. Its every element was part of a unified, intelligent whole, creating a unique holiday venue that had been popular in the periods just before and after the Great War.

Manning's architecture and Gravette and Priest's designs incorporated the ideas and principles of the art deco movement, blending them with, in particular, Gravette's ideas of art as a reflection of what he called 'the lived life'. Aided by Priest's skills in the use of pattern and intricate textile work, Gravette's intense, layered artwork utilised images from both the natural and industrial worlds, turning the *Grand* into a building that was, in a review of the time, "simply astonishing" and which celebrated both mankind's move towards an industrialised society and the supremacy of the natural world. Guests in its heyday found themselves surrounded on the ground floor by designs that were solid, geometric, echoing the patterns found in the factories of the time. On the first and second floors, the designs became more fluid, twisting and losing their angles, and by the third floor, nature had taken over. Here, every element of the decor and the original furniture had implied a triumphant natural world, burying the industrial world's edges beneath the flows and sweeps of leaf and coastline and animal. The *Grand* was unique, and strangely subversive.

As he walked up the tattered staircase to the third floor, Parry couldn't help but smile. Gravette and Priest had been lovers at the time of the hotel's design and construction, and throughout the building elements of that sexuality, slipped in below the radar of the rail company executives, were apparent. It wasn't subtle even; Parry had seen photographs of the missing mural that had adorned the foyer. Across the four sections, a vast and dark locomotive had strained, its windows filled with pale and crammed faces. The train was, in the leftmost panel, erupting from a copse of twisting, stunted trees, and in the rightmost was burying itself into a tunnel whose dark brickwork was surrounded by a collar of white. Celebrated at the time as a grand depiction of the reach and the power of the rail industry, it was in actuality a huge cock disappearing into a vagina. The white collar was a not-very-subtle reference to Priest, the stunted trees Gravette's own pubic hair. *How had they missed it?* mused Parry as he wandered the corridors. *How had they not seen?*

"So what's left?" asked Mandeville that evening. A small lamp illuminated the three men; takeaway pizza boxes littered the floor between them. Around them, Parry's lists were piled, now covered in notations and scrawled comments.

"The carpets are all gone," said Parry. "I can't find any of the original ones, although that's not a surprise, I don't suppose. Most of the rooms have been refitted, so none of the original furniture's left, although rooms 212 and 208 have the lamp fittings in the wall. The bathrooms on the second floor were torn out in the 60s, so we know that all that's gone, but the suites on the third floor still have the original baths with the bath taps."

"Are they the ones shaped like breasts?" asked Yeoman.

"Not breasts, octopi," said Mandeville, smiling.

"Whatever," said Yeoman, also smiling. "They look like tits to me."

"They're supposed to," said Parry. "The third floor suites are all about sexuality, about sex and it being the driving force in nature. Octopi suited Gravette because he could mould the taps to look like their bodies and still have it represent the female form. Priest's form, to be precise. His own form was there in the long lines of the taps' stems. It's all over, the male and female, Gravette and Priest. This whole place is a shrine to them, to their love."

"Did they really fuck in every room on the third floor before the hotel opened?" asked Yeoman, which made Parry grin broadly.

"That's the rumour. They called it 'christening the hotel', according to Manning's diary."

"What else?" asked Mandeville, bringing back the discussion of the hotel's current state, knowing that Parry could happily talk about the history of a place for hours, and that Yeoman would encourage him just because he could.

"The first floor sun deck is pretty solid," said Yeoman. "I went up after I got the camp sorted. It's just a reinforced roof space, but the walls have still got designs etched into them. Waves, by the look of it, although I'm fairly sure I made out fish and fins and things like that. It's pretty faded."

"That was Manning," said Parry, checking a sheet. "He worked with Gravette and Priest pretty closely, but he didn't do much in the way of decoration. It's good that the sun deck still exists; it'll probably be the only bit by him left that isn't the actual structure. He was a big believer in the energising power of the sun, though, and the benefits of a bracing sea atmosphere, so he insisted on having his own designs in the area of the sun lounge. Can you imagine all those rich men and their wives lying on stripy deckchairs in the chilly British summer? Overlooked by the people on the second and third floor?"

"Was he another mucky one?" asked Yeoman.

"No," said Parry, either not hearing or choosing to ignore the humour in Yeoman's voice, "he was tightly buttoned by all accounts, but got on surprisingly well with Gravette and Priest. They believed in the same things, ultimately, in the human body and the power of the natural world. They liked fucking; he liked sunbathing."

"So where do we concentrate?"

"We need a full inventory," said Parry, "but the third floor's the least changed. There's panels covering the walls between the room doors, which might mean they were protecting artwork. The contemporary reports aren't very clear about what was actually done to protect the art and I didn't want to remove a panel without help."

Mandeville made a note on his workplan. Gravette had designed and created two large murals, one for the reception and another for the restaurant that depicted scenes of men, women, animals and machines existing in verdant landscapes of greens and blues. Both were gone, although his smaller pieces were hopefully still inset into the third floor corridor walls. Mirroring the Stations of the Cross, the fourteen small panels showed mythological scenes re-imagined so that in every piece the nude figures of gods and people moved around animals and plants. It would be a real bonus if the fourteen still existed and could be restored and incorporated into the new decorative scheme. *Tomorrow*, he thought. *We start finding out tomorrow.*

Mandeville couldn't sleep. It was partly that his camp bed was uncomfortable and that both Parry and Yeoman snored, but it was also excitement; the *Grand* was the most important job the crew had ever taken on, and it could make their reputation. Most of their earlier work had been in helping homeowners discover the histories of the buildings they lived in and to carry out refits and rebuilds taking this history into account, but the *Grand* was a step into the next league. The art alone, even if only a part of it could be rescued, would add to their understanding of how art had changed and grown in the early years of the century, and the building itself was, in design and construction, almost unique and certainly one of the few surviving examples of its type.

Restless, he walked through to the sun corridor but could see little through the glass. He heard the sound of the ocean crouched in the darkness, muted and elastic like the breathing of some huge animal at rest. It was cold and he pulled his coat tightly around him, watching as his breath misted on the glass in front of him, bleeding to odd colours because the thin coating of paint smeared across the inside of the panes. *I forgot the ask Parry about that*, he thought briefly and made a mental note to do so before they started work tomorrow. When he played the narrow beam of his penlight across the pane, the smears of paint were clearer than they had been in daylight. For a moment, he couldn't tell what the smears reminded him, and then it came to him; it looked as though the windows were covered in hundreds of handprints.

Yeoman whistled as he worked, knowing the sound would reach throughout the building. At some point in the near future, Parry would go and turn on the radio that was sitting on the floor in the middle of the foyer to drown him out, but for now he was enjoying the idea that something of him was filling this place, swooping along the corridors and entering the rooms, tuneless and sharp though it may be.

Parry was somewhere on the first floor, he thought, and Mandeville was recording the art that remained on the ground floor, noting the missing or badly repaired sections of Priest's tiled floor on which they slept at night. Yeoman himself was in the bar that emerged from the rear of the building over the restaurant. Panels of dark wood, designed but not carved by Gravette, lined the walls. Some were warping and sagging, and he was trying to ascertain whether the problem lay with the walls themselves or simply the panels. His initial thought was that it was the panels; each was hanging loose from the walls, the wood twisting and buckled so that the figures carved on their fronts (animals, mostly, their mouths and eyes made oddly angular so that they appeared almost robotic) seemed hunched and wretched. As he leaned in to get a better look at the wall, Yeoman placed his hand on one of the panels, holding it steady away from the wall so that he could angle his torch into the space behind it. The concrete seemed fine; dank, certainly, covered mould spores that probably indicated some minor damp problems, but essentially sound and with no sign of cracking. He started back from the wall, pushing his hand against the panel for leverage, and was alarmed to feel it give around his fingers. The wood, strangely soft, separated and his fingers descended into warm, damp semi-solidity.

Warm? Everything else in the hotel was cold and damp. Yeoman pulled, but his hand remained stuck; he pulled again, wincing as he thought of Mandeville's face when he told him that he'd accidentally pushed his fingers through a piece of artwork. The wood was tight around his fingertips, still warm, but there were splinters in there as well, sharp and needling. He pulled again and then, when his fingers still were not released, he pulled a last, forceful, time.

Mandeville had gridded and completely mapped the floor in the restaurant and was taking a rest. His eyes ached from trying to plot the precise positions of the missing or replaced tiles, almost two hundred of them, on a copy of Priest's original plans. It was a job made more difficult because, in the bright sunlight, the pattern, despite its disruptions, seemed to swirl in a constant half-seen movement, black eyes and mouths forming at the corner of his vision and then breaking up again, only to reform moments later. *Imagine eating with this under your feet*, he thought, *it'd be like floating on the surface of water in which huge fish swam and kept breaching and peering at you!* He started to laugh, seeing the three camp beds pushed back against the wall and a vast leviathan emerging from under the floor and swallowing him and Parry and Yeoman whole as they slept.

Something clattered in the foyer.

It was Parry, Mandeville assumed, come to turn the radio on to drown out Yeoman's whistling, although the architect had actually stopped his tuneless noises several minutes earlier. He waited for the music or inane DJ chatter to begin, but nothing came except another clatter and then the sound of rapid footsteps. Sighing, he got to his feet and went to the doorway, expecting to find some trick or joke being prepared or having already been enacted; Parry and Yeoman were his friends, and were the best men he had ever worked with, but they wound each other up and let the tension out in bickering and jokes and tricks. Sometimes, it was funny; more often, it was childish and irritating. The foyer, however, was empty.

Well, not empty. The radio was lying in the middle of the floor, no longer standing but on its back, its power cable tangled into a black knot next to it. The floor around it was covered in footprints, scuffed and indistinct in the old dust. At first, Mandeville thought that the prints were from Parry or Yeoman, but something about them made him reassess. There were lots, overlaying each other, small and with their edges bleeding into each other, making the floor around the radio into a manic dance chart.

Small?

The prints were small, and neither Parry nor Yeoman was a small man. These prints were much smaller than any he or his colleagues would make. They were narrow, short, a different shape to their own footwear. Experimentally, he placed his foot in an unmarked space and pressed it down hard. When he lifted it, he saw a faint impression of the diamond pattern of his boot sole pressed into the grime. The other footprints were far clearer, as though their makers had trodden in something before walking around the radio. Mandeville pressed his fingers into one of the prints. His fingers came away smeared with dirt that smelled of something familiar, although he couldn't remember precisely what. Some of the prints appeared to trail back towards the staircase and he went to the bottom step, peering up and wondering. If it wasn't him or Parry or Yeoman, then there was someone, several someones actually, in here with them, and judging by the size of the prints, the someones were probably kids.

Mandeville cursed under his breath. It was to be expected, of course; closed-up buildings like the *Ocean Grand* attracted different groups of people who wanted to get inside; aside from historians and urban creepers, kids were the commonest intruders-with drunks and vandals close behind--and they could be a pain. If they had kids breaking in, the likelihood was that they'd damage the place, they'd piss in the corners or set fires, maybe try and steal from the crew's equipment or belongings. They'd have to be found and turfed out, he thought. He'd need to pull Parry and Yeoman back from the jobs they were on and they'd need to do a systematic search of the hotel. Damn, damn, *damn*.

Before Mandeville could call his colleagues, however, Yeoman appeared from the bar, holding one hand out in front of him. The hand was dripping blood, bright in the musty surroundings, and in a tone that was almost conversational, he said, "The fucking thing bit me!"

Yeoman refused to go to hospital, despite Parry's insistence that the slash across his fingers needed stitches. Instead, he made Parry bind each of his injured three fingers with gauze from their first aid kit and take painkillers and told Parry to stop nagging him.

The wounds were messy, punctures that had torn sideways, elongating the openings in his flesh into a series of ragged-edged striations between the first and second knuckles of his middle fingers. They bled heavily, slow to clot despite the pressure that Parry put on them, ripping open as soon as Yeoman moved his hand. Fresh blooms of blood soon soaked the bandages covering his fingers, and by the time the three men came to eat their evening meal, Yeoman had gone through three sets of dressings. Food that night was pizza again, collected by Mandeville from one of the seafront takeaways, and over it they assessed their progress.

"There were two sorts of art here," Parry was saying as they finished their food, "what Gravette called 'integral' and 'peripheral'. The integral stuff is the panels, the floors, the stuff that was built in from the beginning. The peripheral is the other stuff, the things that could be moved or changed: hanging pictures or chairs or the types of plates used. From Gravette's perspective, the whole place was art, and everything in the building was supposed to add to the feeling of being inside a piece of living, breathing, functional art, from the taps that looked like octopi or tits to the colours they used in the original carpet. The peripheral stuff has mostly gone, although we have records of some of it from the original design plans and in photographs, so what we're looking at here is the integral, about 50% of which is still here as far as I can tell.

"The top corridor is the best bet, although a lot of what should be there is hidden at the moment. Tomorrow we'll take the boards off and see what state it's in, but the rooms are mostly intact. The bar and sun deck are pretty much in their original state, although some philistine has replaced the pumps in the bar, probably in the sixties."

"Gravette designed the pumps?" asked Yeoman.

"He designed *everything*. Well, he and Priest did, letting Manning in because they needed his technical skills for the building itself. I keep telling you, this whole place was a testament to Gravette and Priest's belief in the supremacy of the natural world over the things man created. The fittings, the art, the colours, all of them were designed to tell people that they were insignificant when faced the grandeur of God's creation. When they wanted to turn the tap on to run a bath or brush their teeth, the richest guests had to caress something that might have been an octopus or a woman's tit. Think of it, all the rich industrialists whose money came from the mechanical and soulless, come to the seaside for bracing fresh air and views of the North Sea having to rub their great calloused hands over brass tits every day and then had their bathwater spurt out of something that could well be Gravette's cock! And when they went into their corridor, they were surrounded by art that only barely hid its message that shagging was the profoundest act a human could engage in behind classical and religious allusions. Even on the sun deck, they were faced with it."

"With what? You said the sun deck was Manning's creation."

"It was, but he couldn't draw for shit apparently, so he had to ask Gravette and Priest to help him. You can't see it when you look at the carvings of the waves straight on, but when the shadows are right, you can."

"See what?"

Instead of replying, Parry got to his feet, lifting the last piece of pizza from one of the boxes. "Come with me," he said, chewing, and led the other two upstairs. Mandeville followed because Parry had an artist's heart and eye and sometimes saw things that he himself did not. When he put the final report together, containing his recommendations to the new owners, Parry's suggestions about the art and what could be done with it would be central to the document.

The sun deck was dark and cold, and the view of the nearby sea was a grey, shifting mass in the night, chilling the air further. "Stand there," said Parry, pointing to the centre of the deck, "and crouch, so that you're the height of someone on a sun lounger. Now, imagine, you're reading a book, maybe having a little drink, and this is what you can see." He pointed his torch beam at the wall, showing the carved indentations of Manning's design: the waves, line etchings of what might have been fish, plants or undersea grottoes.

"Now," said Parry, "watch the shadows." He began to move his torch slowly around in an arc, travelling over the carvings. Shadows caught in the etched lines and then spilled over, stretched, blossoming into black patches like moss on the wall. Mandeville did not see anything unusual and was about to say so when Yeoman said, "Holy shit!"

"No, holy vagina, technically," said Parry, and Mandeville was about to ask why when he saw it, too. The lengthening shadows reached a point where they combined with the lines of carving and the image changed, danced into something new, a stylised picture of a woman's legs, curved and invitingly open. As Parry kept moving the torch, the image wavered and then vanished, collapsing back in on itself and reforming into waves and sea creatures. "There," he said triumphantly. "Even out here, this place is about being surrounded by femininity, by procreation. By sex. By *life*."

"We have got to recommend that they re-etch these," said Yeoman, laughing.

"Absolutely," said Parry without pause, "and don't tell them why." Mandeville could only nod in amused agreement. Already a plan was forming for the report, where he would recommend the restoration of the hotel back to its original state, using modern artists to fill in the gaps. He was thinking about how to word and present his proposals as they walked back down to the restaurant, his head filled with the possibilities of this place, and it was only later he remembered about the children.

The thought actually pulled him back to consciousness as he was drifting off to sleep, lying wrapped in his sleeping bag on his travel cot. In all the excitement of Yeoman's fingers, and then eating and catching up, he had completely forgotten the intruders. Now he remembered them, though, the thought that they hadn't checked the hotel for obvious entry points wouldn't leave him alone. The *Grand* had survived its locked-up years surprisingly well, with little damage apparently done by vandalism. There was definitely evidence that people had broken in, he had seen it: a pile of old food cartons in the kitchens, a blackened circle in one of the bedrooms that might have meant a small fire had burned there, but there was no real damage. Most of what had broken or collapsed had done so as a result simply of time and the salted coastal atmosphere, of dampness and neglect and air closed in on it-self, trapped and rotting. But still, he should check. Kids, once they found an entrance, could be persistent and destructive. Sighing, he clambered out of his sleeping bag and slipped on his boots and a thick jumper; he was sleeping in his jeans and shirt anyway, to ward off the chill air. His breath misted in front of his face as his tied his laces, and he wondered about waking Yeoman and Parry up to help him, but both were snoring and he decided against it. Yeoman had been weary by the time he fell asleep, his fingers clearly causing him pain. Parry, he knew from uncomfortable experience, was terribly grumpy if woken before he thought he ought to be. He would scout around himself and if he found anything, they could call the security service tomorrow and get them to deal with it.

In the near-complete darkness, Priest's flooring seemed to shift and swirl under him, tracking him in shades of luminal grey as he walked from the makeshift camp to the foyer. His footsteps were gritty, fractured things, his breathing loud, and there was someone standing in the sun corridor.

They were only a shape in the darkness, pressed against the glass with their arms stretched out as though supplicant to the grey swathe of beach and sea beyond. Surprised, Mandeville stopped. The figure did not move. After a moment, he began to approach them cautiously, listening; they were singing, low and wordless, crooning something that might have been a lament or a lullaby, and they were scratching their fingers against the glass. The sound of it was carrying, sharp above the song, setting Mandeville's teeth on edge. The figure was female, he thought, certainly long-haired and curvaceous around the buttocks and thighs, and wearing some kind of long dress or coat that swayed as she moved.

Standing in the entrance to the sun corridor, perhaps fifteen feet from the intruder, Mandeville stopped again and watched her. She was pressed up against the glass, flattened against it, her hair hanging down the sides of her face so that he couldn't make out her features, just a veil of thick tangles that seemed to catch the distant lights from outside and glitter a myriad colours. Her outstretched arms were fully extended, reaching above her and her hands were splayed out, hooking against the pane, and she was still singing. Close to, he could almost hear words in the song, muffled and lost. Her lips and nose had to be pressed hard against the glass as well, he realised. Perhaps that was why her voice was so muffled, seemed to be coming from so far away. This didn't seem like normal vandal behaviour, he thought. Perhaps she was ill? If so, she might need help. "Hello," he said quietly.

The girl spun rapidly, fleeing Mandeville and running down the sun corridor at high speed. Startled, it took him a moment to follow, wondering fleetingly as he did how she had managed to leave an image of herself printed on the glass and why it was so smeared and shot through with wide sweeps of colour.

The girl disappeared down the sun corridor and Mandeville went after her. When she reached the far end, she ran through a second doorway into, if he remembered rightly, what had been a games room. By the time Mandeville reached it, the girl was nowhere to be seen, but he instinctively ran through the room and out into the corridor, turning back towards the reception area. Something skittered through the shadows ahead of him, telling him that he had guessed correctly, and then he was into the reception, its floor crossed by the weak light falling through the iron lattice of the glass roof far above him. He expected to find the girl here, but there was no sign of her.

Mandeville slowed, confused. The nearest staircase started at the far side of the reception area, and even if she'd made it there, the girl should have still been visible on the stairs. There was nowhere for her to hide except behind the reception desk, but a quick check told him that she wasn't there. The main door was still shut and locked; he checked it with a shake. Turning, he peered up the stairs and saw movement in the murky depths of the bar. *How did she make it up there without me seeing?* he wondered as he started to climb the stairs. *She must have moved like a fucking gazelle!*

Whoever it was he had seen wasn't there now. The bar was deserted, the floor as empty of chairs and tables as it had been for years. As he cast his torch beam around, the only movement was the warped wooden panel hanging loose from the wall rocking slightly, as though moved by a breeze. Mandeville peered behind the bar, but the mirrored walls reflected only dust and empty shelves. The wooden panel swayed again, leaning drunkenly out from the wall, held by two of its fittings, the other two dangling loose, the screw threads clenching torn shreds of wood and plaster. It was the panel that Yeoman had caught his fingers on, Mandeville saw; that he had said had bitten him. Parry had ribbed him mercilessly about it after binding his fingers, particularly when they found a torn string of skin caught in the lion's mouth on the front of the panel. Dried blood was still crusted around its mouth, dribbling down its chin and the rest of the panel in long, clotted strings.

Mandeville went back across the bar, flicking the torch around him as he went. Nothing. The girl had either gone further down the corridor, which he doubted, as all the doors along it were locked except the very furthest, to an exit to the fire stairs that squealed violently if it was opened, or she had gone higher, to the second or third floor. This was becoming annoying and complicated, and he would have to wake the other members of the crew to help look for her.

As he reached the doorway, a noise came from behind him: a throaty, hoarse growl that stretched for seconds, and as he turned a dark shape came across the floor at him with a rapid, ferocious clatter.

Yeoman woke to find himself staring at a warped wooden lion, blood flaking from its mouth in dark red drifts. "It fell off the wall last night," said Mandeville by way of explanation, "and nearly gave me a fucking heart attack. Maybe it's got it in for us, what do you think? By the way, we've got an intruder, or at least, we did last night. Somewhere there's a place to get in that we don't know about, and the first job today is to find it."

It was colder than usual that morning, and even dressed and with coffee and breakfast (cooked on the tiny camping stove) inside him, Yeoman shivered. Outside the temperature continued to drop, and as he walked the perimeter of the *Grand* smoking and looking for potential entry points, Yeoman tried to see the hotel as it might be in the future. Architecturally, he considered it sound, so most of his work was done. He had some suggestions to make about the use of the lower floor rooms and about how some of the walls could be altered to make a more open space, but he knew that his role here had become one of support rather than leading. This job would bear Parry's and, especially, Mandeville's stamp rather than his own. He was fine with that, knowing that he would get equal credit anyway; Mandeville was strict about the fact that the members of the *Save Our Shit Crew* were equal partners. Whatever fortune they shared, they shared in equal proportion.

There were no obvious entry points that Yeoman could see, and Parry told the same story from his search of the hotel's insides. Mandeville himself didn't look convinced, but didn't argue, telling them instead to keep an eye out and to be alert. He was distracted, Yeoman knew, because once the search was done they could reveal the third floor's secrets.

"The rooms are intact," said Parry, unnecessarily. They had discussed this already, but he looked as nervous as Mandeville. "Whatever other idiocies the various owners inflicted on this places, they knew that keeping the suites on the third floor as close to their original state was important. The carpets have gone, of course, but we have the patterns for them in Priest's records, so they can be recreated, the wall hangings likewise. The taps, the window latches, the door handles, the bath feet and the fittings for the showers and toilets are all original except for one or two replaced items, but they can be easily sorted out. The carpet in the corridor has been replaced as well, and we don't have a pattern for it, but we do have photographs and descriptions, so recreating it might be complicated, but it's achievable. The theme is all there, waiting for the new owners to agree it, but it only works if the art itself still exists. It's the thing that ties it together, gives the guests the language to understand what their rooms were telling them." Parry spoke like this when he got excited, Yeoman remembered, talking about art's 'language', its 'voice', its 'pulse' and its 'heartbeat'.

"If it's survived, we can recommend that the top floor is recreated in its entirety; that the new guests can be as surrounded by Gravette and Priest's beliefs in God and nature as interchangeable beauties as their predecessors were. If it's damaged, irreparable, then it doesn't matter, the heart will be gone."

As he spoke, Parry was levering the first of the cheap panels from wall. The screws came unwillingly from the wood with a noise like cats in the darkness. The panel, a composite of some sort, bowed out damply, splintering apart as Mandeville took hold of it. "Shit," said Mandeville quietly; the panel was so damp his fingers were leaving denting grooves in it, "they didn't even use decent fucking wood. In this atmosphere. . ." He voiced tailed off, miserable in the silence, as Parry removed the last screw to reveal the first of Gravette's pieces.

It was a picture of a woman standing on the edge of a great sea. She was naked, her back to the canvas, her buttocks and shoulders clearly delineated by Gravette's loving brush, her hair long down her back. Although there was nothing obvious, something in the way the brushstrokes, still visible in the thick paint, formed the sea and the sky hinted at things below the surface or just beyond vision, things that swirled and glided and floated. Around the woman, by her feet on the sand, pieces of machinery lay glittering with oily life, cogs and levers and panelling and rivets forming a platform that looked like a vast mechanical hand upon whose edge the woman was precariously balanced. The picture was, despite the damp affecting the panel covering it, in remarkably good condition. Apart from a small amount of blackly furred moss just creeping along a part of the picture's bottom edge, there was no obvious damage; the colours were bright, vibrant, the detailing astonishing. The woman's muscles were distinct beneath her skin, her outstretched hands seeming to grasp at the whole of the scene beyond her. "Beautiful," breathed Mandeville, and Parry simply nodded. Yeoman, less moved by the artwork but still appreciating the skill that had rendered the picture, said, "Is that Priest, then? Nice arse."

"It's not Priest," said Parry, ignoring the obvious provocation, "it's woman, an archetype, a feminine ideal."

"It's an ideal arse," agreed Yeoman, grinning at Parry. Parry, shaking his head disgustedly but unable to prevent himself also grinning, said, "Let's do the others."

All fourteen pictures were in similar condition, having survived far better than Mandeville could have hoped. Collectively, the pictures were called *The Stations of the Way*, and if you followed their story, up one side of the corridor and then back down the other, right side along and left back, they told the story of Gravette and Priest's beliefs as surely as any bible or philosophical tract. Across the pictures, the woman waded into the ocean, leaving the machinery behind, swimming and dancing with vast and unnameable creatures under the green surface before being lifted out and hauled into the sky by flying versions of the same creatures. The figure of the woman became smaller and smaller in the pictures, surrounded by winged and tentacled and finned creatures with fierce and unforgiving faces but who robed her and held her as, in the distance, small and insignificant, machines ploughed the surface of the water and left tiny trails across the sky. Despite her diminishing size, the woman remained the absolute focal point in each picture, and every one of the creatures in the picture laid their full attention upon her.

The inhabitants of the Grand; The End of the Crew

Although they hadn't finished the job of assessing the *Grand*, Mandeville went out for champagne and the three men drank it that night from plastic cups after they had finished another takeaway meal. They had spent the evening photographing the pictures, making careful notes of any damage they found, and then had recovered them, this time with plastic sheeting. As they had covered the last of the pictures, Parry had said, "Sorry, ma'am, but you can come out again soon."

Mandeville had never seen Parry so excited. "Do you understand how important this is, that they've survived? Gravette and Priest, they were both fine artists in their own right, but this was considered by both to be their crowning glory, and it's still here, and we can make it public again! As you move up through the levels of the hotel, you pass from the mechanised glories of the manmade world on the ground floor, through human pastimes, hunting and drinking and sunbathing, on the first floor. If the second floor had been left alone and not torn apart, we'd have found art that showed men and women abandoning their earthly pursuits, their clothes, work, so that by the time we hit the third floor we're returning to an understanding that all of life is about the worship of nature and a recognition of its power, its *supremacy*. Do you know that through most of the sixties, seventies and eighties, the pictures on the third floor had other pictures hung in front of them? That they were considered 'old-fashioned' and out-dated? What a fucking travesty, all that beauty and life trapped behind crappy prints and photographs of misty fucking landscapes and Victorian watercolours, desperate to be free, and we can do it, we can free it, let it out, let it be loved again!"

"Well, the owners can, if that's what they want to do. All we can do is make the suggestion and try to persuade them," said Mandeville.

"Persuade them?" said Parry. "Force them! They *have* to. We have to make them! It can't stay hidden anymore, it was made to be looked at, created to be seen. They *have* to."

"We'll try," said Mandeville. "Trust me, we'll try."

Mandeville was woken by footsteps. Bleary, champagne-heavy, he forgot he was wrapped in a sleeping bag and on a cot and tried to roll, falling heavily to the floor. The shock jolted him fully alert, and as he struggled to his knees, he listened. They weren't footsteps, not exactly; they were too rapid, too light, and seemed to come from all around the room, from two or three places at once. It was dark; the only light a digital glow from the clock and the glimmer from the extension cable's unblinking LED eye. At the edge of the pale illumination, a darkness shifted, bled out into the shadows around it and formed again, low and cautious. Another patch moved on the far side of the room, easing in through the entrance from the sun corridor. Mandeville freed his arms from his sleeping bag and unzipped it, stepping out and fumbling for his boots. As his hand found them, one of the patches moved again, slinking around the edge of the room. Now the noise was slower, still light, like pencil tips tapping a wooden desk. Mandeville risked looking down for a second to slip his boots on, Priest's patterned floor turning sinuously beneath his soles, and when he looked up, the two patches had been joined by a third.

Parry's cot was empty, but Yeoman was sleeping soundly on his. Mandeville hissed at him, leaning over to shake him when he didn't wake. Even as he leaned, the flowing, creeping patches of darkness, somehow blacker than the shadows around them, began to come in closer, still circling. He shook harder.

"What?" mumbled Yeoman.

"Be quiet," said Mandeville softly, "and wake up. *Now*. There's something in here."

"Something?" asked Yeoman loudly. His breath smelled of cigarettes and sour air and tiredness.

"Something," repeated Mandeville. "Three somethings, actually. Look."

Yeoman sat up in bed, rubbing his hands through his beard with a noise like sandpaper rustling. Whatever it was circling the room, they reacted to the noise, coming in closer, still just out of reach of the light, still mere blackness against blackness, moving with an increasingly rapid *tactactactac* sound.

"What the fuck?" said Yeoman, finally seeing them. "What are they?"

"Don't know," said Mandeville. "Have you got the torch?"

"Yeah," said Yeoman and began rooting on the floor. Finally, with a muffled grunt that might have been the words 'found it', he emerged holding the large lantern torch they used at night. The things were moving faster and faster around them, passing each other, getting lower, still impossible to see other than the *movement*, the rapid circling centering in on the two men, purposeful and raw. There was a click as Yeoman turned the light on, the beam at first glancing into Mandeville's eyes and then upwards, leaving him dazzled, before dropping and gleaming out into the room, catching in its gaze the things that moved about them.

Yeoman screamed.

Mandeville fled as things that could not be, impossible things, came streaking across the space between them and Yeoman in a matter of seconds, brown and lithe in the jerking, spastic light from the torch, and descended on the man. As Mandeville reached the entrance to the sun corridor, the man shrieked, once, the sound cutting off with a noise like tearing paper.

The sun corridor was deserted, silent apart from the frenzied fall of his own feet, and Mandeville ran. The large panes were covered, he saw, in blurred silhouettes, arms outstretched as though trying to embrace the world beyond, overlapping and chaotic, a silent audience for his flight. Ripping sounds danced around him, roars and snarls and, once, a sharp, heavy *crack*, and he ran faster. Through the empty games room and out, along the corridor and into the foyer towards the door, but he was already too late, one of the shapes was there before him, drained to a grimy sepia by the light from above them except around its mouth where a rich redness pooled and dripped. It came from the restaurant, cutting off his passage to the main door, forcing him to shift direction, to go towards the stairs. He hit them in a stumbled run, leaping two or three at a time as the thing streaked towards him, emitting a noise like an escalating fire siren. Its feet (*claws*, he told himself, disbelieving, *they're claws*) skittered as it ran, the nightmarish *tactactactac* getting closer and closer.

At the top of the stairs, Mandeville hesitated briefly. The bar was open ahead of him, but he would be trapped in there. The panel that had nearly fallen on him was leaning in the doorway where he had propped it earlier in the day, its face now blank, the wood smooth and unsullied. The *tactactactac* was getting louder behind him, closer, the fire whistle sound of the impossible thing's growling surrounding him, and then there was light from above him.

It wasn't light, though, not really; more a kind of greasy glow that clung to the walls, dripping from above him, from the upper flights of stairs, from above the second floor in the shadows that clung to the opening of the third floor. In the opening, the darkness seemed to close itself up like a fan, solidifying into a figure that emerged from the doorway, waving at him. He started towards it and then, shrieking, the thing from below was on him.

Despite the champagne, Parry couldn't sleep. Even when Yeoman started snoring (which, oddly, he found a reassuring rather than an irritating sound), he found himself lying awake, teasing at something. He couldn't work out what it was, not exactly; they'd uncovered the pictures that formed the *Stations of the Way* and found them in almost perfect condition, so he should be celebrating, yes?

No.

Something about the top corridor, about this whole place, bothered him. Despite what he had said earlier, flushed with success and alcohol, he wasn't sure about recreating Gravette and Priest's masterwork in its entirety. It seemed too intense, almost extremist in its views; it was *everywhere*, when you looked. From the panels and pictures on all the floors to the design of the taps to the carpeting along the corridors (which no longer existed but which pictures showed had consisted of a complex paisley pattern of interlocking, swirling stems and buds that Priest had called 'cunts and pricks' in one of her notebooks), this place wasn't so much a homage to the supremacy of life and procreation over industrialisation as it was a proselytisation of it.

The *Stations of the Way* was a good example: taken by itself, it was simply a series of pictures that between them formed a narrative, one of returning to recognise the beauty of nature and God's place within it. The religious allegory was unsubtle, and the pictures themselves beautifully done, some of Gravette's best work. But, read another way, they were something more. Gravette and Priest had fucked in every room on the third floor once the pictures were set in place, and there were persistent rumours that Gravette had mixed his semen and Priest's menstrual blood into his paints. Early sketches showed that the original ideas for the *Station* pictures were far more graphic, with the angels of sea and air having sex with the woman, transporting her to God's side in a storm of sexual energy and passion and lust.

The woman. It was the woman in the pictures that bothered him, he suddenly realised. Getting out of his sleeping bag, he pulled on his shoes and went to his untidy pile of folders and photocopies and prints. The problem was that the art in the *Grand* hadn't ever been formally catalogued, and most of it wasn't recorded anywhere, so his research had, by necessity, been forced to travel circuitous routes to find the information they needed. As well as Gravette's and Priest's notebooks, he had scoured old newspaper articles, private photograph collections and what little television appearances the *Grand* had made to try to get an accurate picture of its insides. Leafing through the papers, he came across the screen grabs from the television documentary about the *Grand's* closure, eight of them that showed in not particularly good detail some of the pictures from the third floor. Looking at them by torchlight, prints from a not very high quality source document, he saw what it was that had been bothering him.

The pictures were different.

The positioning of the characters within the pictures was the same, their layout and structure unchanged, but the woman and the creatures that surrounded her were definitely altered. Christ, had someone removed the originals, replacing them with fakes? Only, that didn't feel right either; the boards covering the pictures had looked to be the originals from the documentary, filmed just after the *Grand* finally closed and the pictures themselves were, he would have sworn, original Gravettes. This made no sense, none. Taking the prints and the torch, Parry went out into the *Grand*.

The pictures were definitely different, every one of them that he could make comparisons for. In the prints he held, the woman and the creatures, both the ones that emerged from the air and the water, were painted as innocents. They had wide eyes, almost perfectly round (*like anime characters*, Parry suddenly thought, wondering if there was a research paper there, looking at the shorthand artists of different ages used to depict innocence and vitality), staring back at the observer as they viewed the pictures. Now, though, that had changed. The woman looked past the viewer: her eyes no longer open wide but narrowed, focused on something over the observer's shoulder. The undersea creatures, although not completely anthropomorphic, had flickers of recognisable emotion painted across their features, mouths twisting in anger or frustration, arms and fins and tentacles curling around the woman not in support but in possessive twists as though holding her back and preventing her from escaping. The later pictures in the series, the ones with the woman being elevated into the sky and surrounded by things that might have been angels, or man's better nature freed from the shackles of the flesh, showed the woman still looking back out of the pictures, still staring at something beyond Parry, beyond the *Grand* itself. The angels looked cold, emotionless, their hands taut upon the woman's body but the expressions on their faces supercilious and dismissive.

Parry had reached the end of the corridor, had studied each of the pictures as best he could in torchlight, and he was convinced that they were the work of Gravette. They were technically skilled, full of subtleties and tight, hidden details that only emerged when you looked at them for longer periods, but they weren't the pictures that had been nailed behind cheap boards of wood fifteen or more years back. Had the owners pulled some kind of switch? But why? What would be the point, when they could have merely taken the pictures? He'd have to tell Mandeville, let the owners know, assuming they weren't already aware of the changes. He made to go back down the corridor when he stopped. Was something moving down there, in the tarlike shadows that pooled along the edges of the floor? And there? There?

Everywhere?

As Parry watched, something glistening detached from one of the pictures and drifted to the floor in the centre of the corridor. It rippled and swelled as it fell, floated really, dancing in the air as more fell from every picture along the corridor. Soon the corridor was full of the things, gossamer and glimmering. Some of them moved along the floor after they descended, slithering to the edges of the walls and joining the shadows, thickening them, making them pulse and bulge. It was oddly beautiful, the descents drifting, slow, tracing gentle parabolas through the corridor before alighting with a touch that appeared as delicate as the spinning of feathers or the kiss of elegant mouths.

Soon, the corridor was full of them, pressing out from the walls, swelled by the arrival of more and more of the things. In the centre of the corridor, the first shape he had seen was now moving, not to the side but away from him, along the carpeted floor towards the stairway. As it went, it coalesced, drawing in seemingly identical shapes that were standing ahead of it. Parry counted three, four, ten, fourteen, and as they merged the remaining moving shape became more solid, more real. Parry made out the curve of buttocks, the sway of full breasts, the outstretching of arms and the opening of hands and then something else was moving.

A long tendril came out of the shadow by Parry's side, solidifying as though it was drawing itself together from the thinner shapes, languidly curling in the air above his head. It tapered down to a delicate point, he saw, trembling as though sniffing the atmosphere. As it broadened, became fatter and *realer*, pale discs emerged across its underside, shivering and clenching wetly. *It's a tentacle,* he thought to himself but before he had time to scream, it had dropped onto him and wrapped around his neck.

It *hurt*, crashing into Mandeville's legs and knocking him to the floor. He braced himself for further attack but whatever it was simply flung him out of the way, growling, and dashed on. It hit the wooden panel leaning just inside the doorway, sending it spinning on one edge before it fell, ending up propped between the two sides of the doorframe, canted at a drunken angle. Where it had been blank before, the wood now contained a carving of a huge jungle cat, not a tiger or a lion exactly, but a creature that was an amalgam of those and others. *Fierce nature*, Mandeville thought wildly, *Gravette's fierce nature, hunted and abused but never cowed.* Would two other panels in the bar be blank if he went in and looked at them? He suspected so.

His legs were bleeding, although the tears in his skin didn't feel deep. Mandeville rolled and then stood, unsteadily, leaning on the wall for support. The panel in the doorway swayed, making the cat's face emerge and vanish into the bar's darkness as though it was rocking back and forth and considering him quizzically. From below, in the foyer, came the sound of a distant train, the noise ascending, dopplering and then muffling within the space of a moment. *Going into the tunnel*, he thought as the noise started again. *In and out, in and out.* The other two cats were there, and God knew what else. He looked back up at the waving figure; it had emerged and was now standing at the top of the stairs, still waving, beckoning him upwards.

It was the woman.

Even in the grey light filtering through the glass ceiling, she seemed to glow all colours, casting her illumination about her the way great art did. And she was great art, he understand suddenly, perhaps the greatest there was. He began to move to her, wincing as he climbed the stairs. Where else could he go?

As he approached, she moved back, returning to the corridor where her glow danced about her like distant, guttering flames. As he reached the corridor entrance, he saw movement beyond her. At the far end of the third floor, almost lost to the darkness that pooled there like spilled paint, Parry was sitting against the wall as a myriad tentacles clenched about him. The largest was wrapped around his neck and pulled so taut that the skin either side of the tentacle bulged, bloody and mottled. The air around Parry was filled with moving, darting shapes, fins lifting and dropping and mouths open wide. As Mandeville watched, a larger shape emerged, conical, mouth agape, and tore into Parry's side, shaking him like a ragdoll, tearing a piece from him and disappearing back into the darkness. Parry twitched spastically, blood spraying from him but not falling to the floor, instead floating around him, breathed in by the fish and the octopi and squid and the things without names that scuttled and bobbed and feasted upon him.

Parry managed to twist his head, despite the ever-tightening arm of the octopus that was wrapped around his neck and whose bulbous body was drifting in the air above him. For a moment he was looking directly at Mandeville, his eyes desperate, and then the contact was gone as he was twisted further around. Mandeville didn't move. After all, what could he do?

There were none of the angels in the corridor, he suddenly realised. Just as quickly the realisation came that they were only metaphors, not alive in the way that the cats, the train that was in fact a prick, or the undersea creatures were. They represented intellect and spirituality, not flesh and lusts and desires and passions and things to worship. They weren't alive in the way that *she* was, the woman.

She was standing in the centre of the corridor, her arms outstretched as though to show him the things that belonged to her, and they *did* belong to her, he saw; they moved around her, never touching her, always giving her space. *It's how they've been painted*, he realised, *to worship her. If she's a female archetype, then those other things are men, sleek and brutal and driven by lust and greed and desire, and between them they make. . .what?*

She was approaching him again now, moving down the corridor as though carried by currents that he could not feel, moving towards him, beautiful and austere. And suddenly he wanted her; he was hard and sweating despite the pain in his legs and the part of him that even now was calling for his attention, was screeching its fear of this impossible situation. She came closer still, her features resolving, streaks forming on her skin in a pattern of delicate brushstrokes. Her hair moved in clumps, strands matted together, *painted* together. Her arms were outstretched and suddenly Mandeville thought about her, about her pressing herself against the glass of the sun corridor, about her seeing the outside world at night and spending most of her time trapped under boards, locked inside the paint, alive and claustrophobic and alone except for creatures without mouths or intellects, just cocks made to love her. How terrible must her life have been these last years, he suddenly thought, trapped here day in night out, with no one to look at her, no one to feast themselves upon her, how awful it must have been.

And what damage had it done to her?

Her face twisted into a snarl as she came, lips drawing back from teeth that seemed suddenly too large and too white and too hard, her arms stretching forward, the skin of her hands broken by paintbrush swirls that reminded

Mandeville of the sucking pads of the octopi and squid that served attendance upon her. Sharks darted between her legs, and still she came and Mandeville saw the hate in her eyes, the desperation to hold him and own him, to take him from the outside and bring him in and keep him so that he, too, could look at her and worship her, and he turned and ran.

The two cats were waiting for him on the stairs between the foyer and first floor, brown and wooden yet terribly fluid, moving back and forth with a restless energy. Trapped between them and her, Mandeville stopped on the first floor and turned a full circle, looking for an escape route. The bar was blocked to him; the third cat still stood in its entrance, back on its board but its mouth open in a rictus of teeth and ravenous appetite. He debated running back to the second floor, losing himself in the place where Gravette and Priest's hold had been comprehensively removed, but the woman was already between him and it. A vast octopus, stretching an impossible height from the floor, moved behind her, its black eyes gleaming, and around it circled the sharks and the smaller fish. She was smiling, possessive, absolute, still coming on, placid and inexorable.

That left only the sun deck.

Mandeville ran to it, crashing against the door and forcing the cheap lock in one stumbled fall of his body weight. One of the cats leaped at him, snagging its teeth into his leg, but its grip was weak and he managed to kick it off. The octopus came past the woman, spreading its arms in an effort to reach him, but he ran, dodging past it and out onto the wooden apron of the deck. He had time to wonder why, if they wanted to get out, the woman and her entourage didn't simply come out here, and then he was at the concrete wall. Its carved pictures moved, writhing and sucking and trying to grasp at him, and then he was over the wall and was airborne.

In the moment before he hit the ground, Mandeville realised; art, true art, has no urge to escape to the outside, it wants instead to bring the outside in, to make itself the centre of a world that it defines. The last thing he saw as he fell past the sun corridor's floor length windows were the myriad images that the woman had left of herself across the inside of the glass, arms outstretched to embrace a world and draw it in, and he smiled. Falling, leaping, escaping, moving on, these were human actions, and in these last moments he had realised: he was human and free to fall.

Nakata 5: Under Great Moore Street, Manchester

The tiles were still in good condition, glimmering in the dimness and reflecting Hammond's torch beam where it fell on them. From floor to about five feet up they were a marbled green colour with veins of pale pink and yellow running through them; above they were much paler, a blue-tinged off-white reaching to a ceiling perhaps ten feet above their heads.

"Clever, isn't it?" asked Hammond, playing his torch up and down. "Restful: oceanic at the bottom, light and airy above. Puts people at the ease, see?"

"Yes," replied Nakata. He could hear the sound of distant traffic, heavy and constant; dust hung in the air, shivering to the vibrations. It smelled in here, of stale urine and dampness and wood blooming with decay, and disinfectant. Was it always this way? The layout, I mean?"

Hammond nodded. "Yes. The cubicles to the left and the urinals to the right at the rear, sinks and the attendant's station here at the front. Here, have you seen this?"

The older man went past Nakata, his high visibility jacket a startling green in the gloom. He pointed his torch at the wall to Nakata's rear. Along the wall were three gaping holes in the tiles, their black maws ringed by the jagged remains of the ceramic squares, spitting plaster dust in long trails to the floor. In among the holes were two urinals, large porcelain cups held on the wall by rusting pipes and stained mortar. Hammond aimed his torch into one of the urinals, pointing it at what Nakata thought at first was a dark smudge. "Look," said Hammond.

Nakata went closer, peering at the smudge. Closer to, he saw it was a small drawing of a bee, glazed into the urinal's curved wall about two thirds of the way up from the drain at the bottom. "It showed the Victorian gentlemen where to aim their flow," said Hammond, laughing, "so as not to get piss spatters on their boots. It's a bee, see? Latin for a bee is 'apis', see?"

At first, Nakata didn't see and then he did, and it made him smile. "Victorians, see? Everyone thinks that they were humourless buggers, but they weren't, they were just subtle. Unexpected, see?" said Hammond. Nakata grinned at him, thinking *It was white and it was screaming and screaming.* He glanced down at the papers in his hand, the printout of the email and photocopies of old newspaper articles, leafing through them until he found the passage he was looking for. *I was at the end urinal, the end near the door, halfway through doing what I needed to do, when I heard a noise. I turned because I knew there was no one else in the toilet, it was locked, and something white came out of the cubicle furthest away. It was white and it was screaming and screaming, and I screamed as well and I ran.*

Nakata went to the end urinal, or at least where it would be if it had still existed, stood in front of it as though urinating, and turned. Swivelling from the waist, the five cubicles were all visible over his shoulder. So it was at least physically possible, he thought. "When did this place have an attendant until?" he asked.

"Just after the second war," said Hammond. "There was an idea that returning soldiers, the cripples, could be given this kind of job, but it cost too much in the end. In the sixties, most of the woodwork was replaced, which is why the cubicle walls are so thin, and these places were pretty much left to their own devices. They were cleaned every few days, unlocked in the morning and locked again at night. Even that finished, though; vandalism got worse, people using drugs. Underground toilets aren't the safest places, either; there were assaults, muggings, people nicking coats and bags, that kind of thing. I suppose there were murders and rapes as well, but not in this one."

It matched what was said in the email, that its author had been the council employee who cleaned and locked and unlocked this toilet between the late sixties and its closure in the late eighties. "And it's been unused ever since?"

"Yes. There was some talk of converting it into a bar, but it didn't come to anything. Only one entrance see, couldn't get a fire safety certificate."

Nakata went to stand in front of the furthest cubicle from the urinal. There was no toilet left in there, simply another black hole in the wall and pipes dangling from an overhead cistern bleeding rust from its base. Stains climbed the walls, stretching up from the floor and opening their arms around the cistern in a dirty orange embrace. Experimentally, Nakata reached a hand into the cubicle; it was cold. *Understandable*, he thought, *there's a hole in the wall.*

He would have ignored the email, except for the fact that its author had signed it. He had also stated his job, where he had worked, dates, verifiable facts that Nakata had checked and was happy with. A quick trawl of the internet had brought up little about the toilet except for some information about its closure, and then some speculative articles about its conversation to the bar Hammond had mentioned. Just an underground toilet and only one report that Nakata had found of anything untoward happening here. Just a toilet.

The other cubicles were warmer, even the ones that also had no toilets and holes in their walls. Nakata put his hand into each, coming finally to the last one in the row. It was definitely colder. As Hammond watched, he licked a finger and extended it, trying to see if there was a breeze that might explain the temperature difference. Nothing. He lit a match, holding it and letting it go out. The flame burned evenly, and the smoke rose straight up, its dance apparently unaffected by any other movement of the air.

Just one incident, *something white and screaming*, just one. *Why am I here?* he thought. *Really? Tidyman? Faith? Hope?* He didn't know, not really. He looked about him, at the cheap woodwork and the tiles that had lasted over a hundred years, at the piled planks lying in the corner near the door, at sinks stained black and orange from water and time and cheap soap. Hammond was looking at him, watching as he walked up and down, investigating each cubicle. What would he think? *That I'm mad*, thought Nakata sourly. *Perhaps I am. So it's cold? So what?*

But it was *cold*, noticeably so, in the last cubicle, and *something screaming and screaming* and what choice did he have? Really?

"I'll need to run a couple of extension cables down here," he said to Hammond. "I suppose that's okay?"

"Of course," said Hammond. "There's power, and it's still connected. I'll arrange for them to be sorted later on today, if that's okay?

"Perfect," said Nakata, thinking, *I'll give it one night, maybe two, and then that's it.*

"Hey, do you know what this place was called?" asked Hammond as he walked back to the worn steps that led up to the outside world.

"No," Nakata replied. "The Great Moore Street Public Conveniences?"

"Not even close," said Hammond. "On the council books, they're actually listed as 'WC212 (abandoned)'. But, see, the Victorians had a name for places like this, this one and all the others. They called them 'The Temples'. Each one had a different name, but they were all The Temple of something or other. There's a Temple of Convenience, a Temple of Joy, a Temple of Acceptance, even a Temple of Difficulty. This one's the Temple of Relief and Ease."

Relief and Ease, thought Nakata as he followed Hammond, *let's hope so. Faith and proof, relief and ease. Let's hope so.*

The cubicle, door missing, exposed and empty, waited.

The Temple of Relief and Ease

The inside of the cubicle was one of three cold spots that Nakata eventually found in the Temple; the other two were in the original attendant's station and in front of the place where the middle urinal had been. The last he could dismiss immediately, as it was caused by the draft coming in from the hole in the wall where the urinal had been, the black maw opening to an inky darkness that his torch couldn't penetrate for more than a few feet. The other two spots, however, he could find no obvious explanation for; they were simply patches of air two or three degrees cooler than the air around them. The edges of the patches were clearly defined, and he could map them by simply moving his arms about and gauging the changing temperature against his skin. Unusually, both cold spots showed up on the heat sensitive camera, darker green patches hovering against pale green surroundings.

Hammond had laid copies of the original schematics for the Temple, as Nakata was now thinking of it, on the floor, anchoring each corner with a piece of broken tile. "See?" he said. " Cubicles here, urinals here, sinks there and at the end of them the attendant's station. Well, they called it a station in the plans, but really it was a chair between the wall and the worktop end. The worktop extends quite a bit past the last sink, see? That's because he'd have had a basket or two of soaps, shoe blacking, dubbin and brushes, piles of towels for the gentlemen to use, that kind of thing."

Hammond had run power cables to the back of the Temple, allowing Nakata to set up his laptop and recorders on a trestle table that Hammond had also brought down for him. At each of the two rear corners, cameras on high tripods peered out, sending constant streams of information to the laptop. Two more were standing at the front of the Temple looking inwards, one pointing at the wall where the sinks had been and the other at the cubicles. Between them, all of the Temple was covered. In addition, separate sound microphones and thermometers were hanging at various points, wires looped around any convenient hook that Nakata could find: the edge of a cubicle, a pipe angling out from a cistern, the camera tripods, all had been brought into service. Nakata was fairly sure he had the best coverage he could get, and he could move the cameras remotely if he needed to, switching between normal film and heat-sensitive imaging. He was set.

"Are you sure you want to stay here tonight?" asked Hammond.

"Well, it's not where I'd spend my night if I had a choice," said Nakata, thinking of all the 'aren't you afraid' questions he was inevitably asked when people found out what he did for a living. "But it's part of the job. Besides, there's nothing to be frightened of." *Something white came out* he thought, and then dismissed it irritably. *Something white, screaming and screaming.*

"Well, if you're sure," said Hammond, his voice low, uncertain. He looked up, to the point where the walls met the ceiling, staring at the grimy light coming in through the thick frosted windows. Occasionally, a blurred shape passed the glass as someone walked along the pavement above their heads. "You're in the middle of the business district, not near bars or clubs, so you shouldn't be bothered by drunks trying to get in after their night out. The police know you're here, but you won't have a mobile signal because we're underground and the walls are thick, so if anything happens, you'll have to go up the steps and get near the door to contact the outside world, see?"

"Yes," said Nakata. "I understand. I'll keep my lights low so as not to attract attention. It'll be fine."

"Yes," said Hammond, walking over to the entrance. Before he went, he placed a set of keys on the trestle table. "The door at the top of the steps can be unlocked from the inside, so I'll lock you in."

"Thank you," said Nakata, glancing at the quartered image on his laptop screen. Four Hammonds, all from different angles, moved across the pictures.

"Are you sure you don't want me to stay? I don't mind, honestly, if you want the company. I'm not saying I've ever seen anything to be afraid of, or that anyone's seen anything here, but these places, they aren't happy, see?" the older man said. "They're places where we got rid of waste, buried it underground and in cubicles like it's something to be ashamed of; and that feeling never leaves places like this, not really. It soaks into the walls along with the piss stains and the smell of shit and cheap soap. Being alone here might not be very nice."

"No," said Nakata, "I'm sure it won't, but I'll be fine, honestly. I've done this before, please go home and relax and I'll see you tomorrow morning. I'll be fine."

I'll be fine, he thought as he heard Hammond lock the outer door. He watched as the man's legs passed in front of the windows, hesitating slightly before they vanished completely, and thought again, *I'll be fine* and tried not to think about white things and screams echoing around the hard, tiled walls in layering, choral waves.

People rarely understood until they experienced it: what Nakata did was, for the most part, boring.

Nakata poured himself a coffee from the flask in his bag, took out his papers and settled back into his chair. Years of doing this, hundreds of nights spent in ancestral homes and hotel lobbies and suburban terraces had taught him three things: bring warm clothes, bring refreshments and bring something to do. The initial adrenaline rush, the clammy hands and beating heart that started as he was left alone would soon fade, leaving only the hours stretching before him like miles of flat, uninspiring road. Survival depended on being prepared, by having faith, by hoping.

Whilst Hammond was sorting out the extension cables and table, Nakata had returned to the university and then home to pick up his equipment. One of the things he had collected was a fat sheaf of additional papers prepared for him by one of the PhD students. There were no stories about this toilet that might be termed supernatural, that was true, but it did have a history, one consisting of people and bricks and urban development and budgets and councils, and he wanted to understand that. The papers were as much as the student had been able to find in the short time he had given her, printouts of minutes from meetings that no one now remembered, of news articles, of reports. There was even, Nakata found, a glossy brochure from some time in the mid-sixties detailing the redevelopment of the area, including promises about restoring the toilet to its "Victorian heyday". Looking at the broken cisterns and the cheap, warping woodwork, he doubted they had ever managed it.

For the first hour, Nakata read. Most of the material was dull, and there were very few pictures. *Why would there be? Who takes pictures of toilets?* he wondered, smiling to himself. One photocopy did have a drawing on it, however, of a smiling-faced man with one arm missing, his suit jacket sleeve pinned up in a way that Nakata thought of as old-fashioned. The picture caught Nakata's eye and he looked more closely at the paper.

It was a tract, he saw, produced by a charity called *The Crippled Man's Support*, detailing the work opportunities that were available for servicemen returning from the Great War whose bodies were not complete. *Jobs are Available!* the tract said cheerily, *as Attendants and Porters and Watchmen and Caretakers!* It went on to explain that the "cripples and deformed can still perform a useful function" and would be paid a fair wage for their services. "We have made arrangements with the councils of Britain to provide them with your labour!" Nakata read, and wondered if that arrangement meant a high income for *The Crippled Man's Support* as well as the men it supported. He suspected it did.

Stapled to the copy of the tract was another set of papers.

Where on earth did she find this? Nakata wondered of the PhD student. The additional papers were the payment record showing that someone called Joseph Tulketh had been paid monthly by the council as the attendant here in the Great Moore Street toilets. The record covered the years from 1919 until 1962, at which point there was an additional payment labelled as 'retirement gift'. The retirement gift was half the amount of Tulketh's monthly wage. *Generous*, thought Nakata.

Nothing moved on the images on the laptop's screen. As the day's light faded, mellowing through murky layers to night, Nakata realised he was reading by the light from the screen and flicked on a small camping lantern he had brought with him. Its glow didn't spread; it gave shape to the corner shadows rather than banishing them. He looked at his watch, knowing that he had only been in the Temple for a couple of hours but hoping it was longer. It wasn't.

Nothing moved, nothing sounded.

Restless, Nakata rose and went over to the entrance to the toilets. *Forty three years*, he thought. *Forty three years here.* Crouching in the space that Hammond had told him was the attendant's station, he looked around the Temple. What was it, really? A single long room, tiled in pale green and with dark wood fittings, carved out underground with little natural light or ventilation. Forty three years watching men piss, hearing them shit, smelling them, cleaning their boots and giving them towels and taking the towels off them when they were done, trapped in a room in which the air was bad and the space small. How had the war affected Tulketh, he wondered? Was he missing an arm like the man in *The Crippled Man's Support's* drawing? A leg? Had the skin in his face been burned into new, puckered patterns of ugliness? Or was it something less obvious, damage written on the inside of his skin rather than the outside?

Someone walked past the Temple, their feet just visible to Nakata through the high windows as moving patches of darkness against the muffled night sky. He heard someone call, another person reply. They sounded happy, as though their meeting was a surprise, a pleasant one. *Forty three years watching the world walk past*, he thought as the legs disappeared, *while down here. . . what?* He didn't know, not really. Sighing, he went back to his chair and poured himself another coffee. More papers waited for him.

It was almost midnight when Nakata noticed that one of the cold spots was expanding.

At first he thought it was his imagination: that the darker green patch hanging in the air in the last cubicle merely looked larger on the screen, but when he scrolled back through the evening's film, he found that it had definitely increased in size. Intrigued, he rose and stretched. Hearing his joints pop, he went to stand in front of the cubicle. The edge of the cold patch was brushing up against him now, whereas earlier it had been contained within the wooden walls; it was colder as well, he was sure. His breath misted in front of him, forming clouds that fell away slowly, dissipating only as they reached the floor.

Back at the table, the thermometers told him that the temperature in the Temple was down a couple of degrees overall; that was to be expected, it was approaching the middle of the night and the toilet had no heating. The temperature in the cold spot, however, was down by nine degrees. Nine degrees!

Nakata couldn't feel a breeze, which was his next idea. Sewers were colder at night, a worker he had once interviewed told him, because they were used less, so there was less warm shit and piss to heat them. Was the lower temperature under the streets, under the Temple itself, causing the cold spot? The hole in the wall where the toilet pipes had entered, carrying the waste away, was certainly chilly when he put his hand to it, but nine degrees chillier? No. He moved one of the thermometers, placing it in front of the hole and found that it was only a degree lower than the average temperature in the rest of the Temple.

Nakata didn't get excited, but this was certainly unusual. First, he checked that his equipment was recording the differences, and found to his satisfaction that they were. A cold spot didn't mean the advent of the supernatural, didn't mean anything precisely, but proof of it might be useful.

The second cold spot was growing as well.

On the monitor, the cold spot in the attendant's station was expanding downwards, stretching out of the oval shape it had been into something new, something elongated and deformed. As it grew, Nakata became aware of a smell, of the flowering of the smell that had filled the temple earlier but that he had stopped noticing a while ago: of human waste.

The first of the cold spots, the one in the cubicle, had filled the space around it and was spilling into the next cubicle. On the laptop screen, it looked like thick, sluggish liquid was pouring over the top of the wooden wall and gathering in coagulating patches. The second patch had now achieved a shape that Nakata almost recognised and was occupying a space from the floor to about three feet in height. When he looked directly into the room, he saw nothing, but on the screen they were clear, moving patches of coldness.

Moving?

Yes, Jesus, yes, moving! Nakata watched, mesmerised, as the speed of the first patch's growth increased, filling all the rest of the cubicles rapidly. Even as he watched, something detached itself from the first cubicle and drifted across along the line of sinks. No, 'drifted' wasn't right, not exactly, it didn't drift, it moved *purposefully*, pausing briefly in front of one of the spaces where the sinks had been and then carrying on before stopping at the second cold patch. After a moment, it continued, finally dwindling and collapsing to nothing as it reached the entrance to the Temple.

By now, each cubicle space was filled with what looked, on the screen, like roiling, murky water. Patches started detaching themselves from the front of each cubicle, overlapping, moving at different speeds, more and more and more, milling in front of the sinks and then carrying on to disappear at the door. Nakata could still see nothing when he looked directly at the sinks or the door or cubicles, but on the screen the shapes were clear.

Nakata couldn't see anything, but he started to hear something, a kind of low murmur. It was like voices that weren't voices exactly, as though hundreds of people's speech was threading apart into tendrils so that there were no words left, only fragments. Sounds gathered in the room, storm clouds of noise that the recorders could hear, their needles jerking and spiking. Nakata looked around again. There was still nothing to see.

On the screen, though, was more movement than Nakata could track, and at its centre was the second cold spot, now a pulsing blackness whose shape reminded him of something, although he couldn't place quite what. He checked again, still unable to quite believe what was appearing on the laptop screen, making sure that the sounds and the thermal images were being recorded. Evidence, safely locked into his hard drive, of something.

Of something. Nakata was trying not to get too excited; he had been here, or in places like it, before, and he knew that whatever evidence he presented would be picked apart by the sceptics and naysayers before it had a chance to convince most people. It would be put down to drafts, to water vapour, to subterranean subsidence, to equipment failure or deliberate hoaxing. He wished he had brought someone with him now, someone unrelated to his work, so that he might have had some independent correlation. Hammond maybe, helpful and concerned and saying, "See? They aren't ghosts, no, we can't say that, but we can say, 'It's very odd and needs more investigating', that's for sure."

The smell of human waste was getting stronger.

It was rank, thick and sour, and Nakata suddenly wished he had some way of recording *this*, so that he could help people understand what these places were like. He glanced down again, watching the constantly moving patches of coldness. What would it be like to stand in them, he wondered? Would he feel them pass him, go through him? Or would they break around him like clouds around a mountain? Was he more real than they or they more real than him? Since Amy had died he sometimes felt like the things he investigated: only half there, less than real. Nakata stood, looking back at the space in front of him. *Show yourself*, he thought helplessly, *show yourself to me. I'm tired of faith and hope; I need proof. Show yourself.*

Nothing. Simply an expanse of wall and the remains of sinks and a marbled surface and tiles whose glaze was yellowed and cracked.

The noises were louder, building, accumulating strata upon strata so that it was becoming a quiet shriek, the smell sitting under it like a counterpoint, an anchor holding it in the room. It was becoming unbearable, choking Nakata, and for the first time he started to worry. He started to move towards the door, lifting the keys from the table as he went, casting one last glance at the screen as he did so. The second cold spot was, if anything, even chillier now, and in a moment of clarity, he recognised what it was its shape reminded him of.

It was a man or, at least, it gave the impression of being male. It wasn't a perfect outline, looking more like one of those time-lapse photographs whose overall shape was clear but whose edges were blurred because of small movements during the hours of the exposure. *No*, he thought, *not hours, years.*

Forty-three years.

Tulketh.

The question was, was it Tulketh or merely a memory of him, built by repetition and recorded in stone and wood and memory? Until recently, Nakata would have said it was merely a memory, an imprint etched into the space in some way they didn't yet understand, but 24 Glasshouse had changed that, the Glasshouse Estate and footsteps crawling through wet grass, following him. Tulketh, still occupying the place he had spent most of his adult life, or a memory of him, a picture painted in tones of chill and damp and odour?

The smell was worse, abrasive, the noises louder, becoming painful. It wasn't the volume so much as their tone, piercing and direct, stabbing at Nakata's ears. It was aggressive somehow, vicious and unpleasant and dismissive all at once. There were still no words in the scree of sounds, just as there were no individual smells in the morass, simply an overwhelming, heady stench of shit and piss and soap and body odour and polish and boredom and despair.

Despair?

Yes, yes, Nakata could feel it, despair, coming out of the corner in waves, carried by the cold and the noise and the smell, a sense of absolute loss, unhappiness, pain and worthlessness. The pressure in the room felt as though it was building as the sounds and smells and feelings filled it, pressing back in on Nakata, forcing him to brace against it. On the laptop screen, the cold patches were no longer separate drifting things but had started to merge in a constant stream, each cubicle letting out a long tendril of coldness that stretched away from the open spaces to the Temple's door, eddying in front of the sinks, and clustering in front of the attendant's station before vanishing.

Something was about to happen.

A voice came out of the noise, sudden and clear, "You! Towel!" and then the babble was reforming, becoming words, questions, orders, conversations and underneath them all another voice, slow and quiet and distinct. "Help you, sir? Pleasure, sir. Of course, sir. Yes, sir," and on and on, unfolding before him, approaching whatever climax there could be.

It was white, and screaming and screaming.

The voice was male, older, ragged around its edges, and absolutely subservient to the babble, fitting itself to the rhythms of the louder noise. Nakata stepped away from his chair, towards the cubicles and away from the urinals, wanting to have the best view of the Temple he could. The coldness had spread, its edge meeting him somewhere in the middle of the room, not a breeze but an *edge*, where the temperature of the midnight air dropped even further so that for one dislocating moment Nakata's rear was warmer than his front and then he was into the chill and it was all about him.

The Temple was full of people.

They were all men, hundreds of them, *thousands*, moving in and out of the Temple, entering and exiting the cubicles, bending at sinks that were restored to their original condition and washing hands, pausing in front of the attendant's station to have their boots cleaned or to take towels, give towels back. They overlapped, merged, separated, passed through Nakata and around him, some smiling, some not. Gooseflesh sprang out on Nakata's skin, the cold bringing it forth and his fear clenching it tighter. These were *ghosts*, the images of people long gone and forgotten, their costumes from the twenties and thirties and forties and fifties, suits and slacks and shirts and ties and jumpers and jackets in an endless stream.

Tulketh was in the corner. He was an old man, his face lined and unshaven and he was dressed in a suit that glimmered with age at the knees and el-bows, shirt collar tight around a neck that was wattled and fleshy. There were stains down the front of his shirt and his left arm was crumpled and misshap-en, hanging across his front, the hand sticking out from his jacket sleeve like the husk of some exotic fruit gone dry and rotten. He was sitting on a chair, looking up at the never-ending movement of men around him, his good arm handing out towels and taking them back, using the shoe brushes, assisting.

Serving.

Nakata thought at first that the expression he saw on Tulketh's face was a happy one, as the man, the ghost of the man, nodded and smiled and carried out his work. As Nakata watched, he became aware of new sounds, that of liquid hitting liquid, of men pissing onto porcelain, of solids hitting water, of men puking, of zips and groans of relief, of flatulence, and as these sounds rose dizzyingly, the smell rose with them. Nakata coughed, the acrid tang of urine catching at the back of his throat, as he looked again at Tulketh. There were two expressions on the man's face, one sitting behind the other: the front benign, the rear miserable and furious. Nakata had the impression that the rear expression was deeper somehow, more truthful. *Forty three years*, he thought again, *and then something white came out* and then Tulketh screamed.

It was terrible, seeming to drag itself up from some deep and raw place. Tulketh's front face flaked away, revealing the rear expression, one of bone-white fury. He lurched out of his chair, flailing at the men around him, tear-ing them apart like damp paper. Tulketh screamed again, his bad arm jig-gling against him. He clawed at himself, tearing open his shirt and shedding it and his jacket in one uneven movement, staggering forwards. His body was old-man flabby: sagging, hairless and pale as he lurched towards Nakata. He was already losing his shape as he came away from his station, becoming a shapeless white mass, screaming and screaming as he came, and Nakata was screaming, too, and backing away but not fast enough and then Tulketh was on him.

There was a moment that was worse than any other Nakata had ever had, worse than Amy's death or her funeral, worse than the first time he slept without her, worse than the moment with Wardle in 24 Glasshouse, worse than all of it. As Tulketh, or whatever it was, hit him, he felt a rising wave of absolute blackness, of misery and boredom and of being wasted and unwanted and an embarrassment, fill him. *They hid him underground,* he managed to think, *where no one could see him, where people ignored him, where he cleared up piss and shit and puke. Where people forgot about him.* The weight of it staggered him, the volume of Tulketh's scream increasing, the smell jamming his nostrils and making him gag. He stepped back and banged into the table, but Tulketh was pressing on, still screaming. Nakata was forced back further, trying to turn so that he could move around the table, but there was no space and instead he was falling.

Tulketh was with him all the way to the floor, pressing and clutching at him, and as the table crashed down around him, the dead man's scream merged with an electronic whine that was abruptly cut off in a dazzle of breaking plastic and glass. Tulketh screamed again, raw and bloody and white, and then he lifted away. For a moment, Nakata had a sense of someone else's freedom, of hope, of *release*, and then it was gone.

The cameras were unharmed, as were the thermometers, but the laptop was lying on its back on the floor, its screen dark. Strings of liquid spilled out from the USB ports on its side, leaking onto the floor around it. The liquid smelled like old urine and excrement.

What had happened here? He didn't know, not really. Tulketh's ghost, appearing like some malignant reminder of how he had been treated in life? His emotions, all of his hate and loathing, soaked into the walls and discharging like a jolt of static electricity? Both? Neither? Without the evidence on the laptop, he could only guess, and he knew without knowing that the laptop would reveal nothing even if he took it to a specialist for repair. Sighing, he closed it, careful not to let the liquid get on his fingers, and put it on the pile of lumber near the Temple's door. Standing by the door, he took his phone from his pocket and saw he had a signal, although only a weak one. He debated ringing Hammond, but decided against it. He was tired, too tired to explain things, too tired to be scared or upset. Instead, he went back to his chair and sat down. He put the papers back in his bag and thought about how to write this up.

It wasn't real, he thought. *It wasn't anything that happened; it was everything Tulketh wanted to happen. If I ask Hammond, or someone else who knows, they won't tell me that Tulketh went mad and attacked someone here, or committed suicide. No, they'll tell me he retired quietly after years of dutiful service and went home to die, as forgotten and ignored in retirement as he had been in employment.*

Nakata pulled a pad and a pen from his bag. Trying to remember everything that had happened, he began to write, thinking, *43 years. Jesus. 43 years, and something white, something white and screaming and screaming and screaming and screaming.*

The Temple was silent apart from the scratching of pen against paper.

Nakata 6: Tidyman's Office

"It's not enough."

Tidyman leaned back in his chair, looking at Nakata. Nakata held his gaze, trained by years of departmental meetings and funding application boards to not let his intimidation show.

"I know," he said. "I told you this might happen. I told you it probably would happen, in fact, that you'd have nothing you could use."

"That's as may be," said Tidyman, "but still, I hoped for more." He gestured at the low pile of paperwork on the desk, and the two men looked at it for a moment; buff folders full of faith and hope and certainty without proof.

"It's not that these aren't fascinating," said Tidyman, eventually. "They are. Each is genuinely interesting, and I'd love to be able to talk about each with you in more detail. We may yet do that, you and I, I hope, one day when this is over. The problem is, these aren't enough to persuade anyone, let alone a judge or jury."

"I know, but there's nothing I can do," said Nakata. He filed away the 'we may yet do that, you and I' for future consideration, but now he had to get through a meeting that was becoming uncomfortable, in which he felt he had disappointed a client. Not that he had expected anything else, of course. How could he, given what Tidyman had asked him to do, what he had failed to do, what he always knew he'd fail to do? He wondered again, not for the first or the tenth or the hundredth time, why he had taken the job on. *Because you thought there was a chance, of course*, he replied, *because of faith, faith and hope, your faith and hope.*

And the money.

"A man's liberty may depend on this, Mr Nakata," said Tidyman. "I appreciate the difficulty of the task I set you, but I'd ask you again, is there nothing else you can add? We're so close with these, but we aren't there yet."

"No," said Nakata, "there's nothing."

"Nothing?" asked Tidyman. "Are you sure? Because I'd say there is. The thing at Heysham, the lavatory incident, these are useful because you have a certain reputation, your word means something. The photographs you have taken of the Merry House exterior are fascinating and odd, Mandeville's statement and the collaborating evidence about the artwork in the hotel is powerful stuff indeed, but it remains simply not enough. There is, however, another thing you were involved in, something which has some externally verifiable evidence, I believe? Something that can, with your permission, provide proof?"

Nakata didn't respond. Tidyman was talking about the Glasshouse Estate, of course; he should have known, should have guessed that this would happen. It had been naïve of him to think that Tidyman hadn't known, a naïve hope and an unrealistic one.

"There's another story you can add, a story with some proof, I think," repeated Tidyman after a taut pause. "Let me be honest, Mr Nakata, and I would urge you to do the same. I know the rumours, and I've read the media and police reports. That testimony, your testimony, I've never understood why you didn't make it more widely available."

"It proves nothing," said Nakata, thinking about the lights coming down the staircase, about Amy, about things going bump in the night, and then in the day. About the things that he'd seen.

"Perhaps not," said Tidyman, "but it surely adds weight to your argument? You have film, I believe? Sound recordings?"

"The police have them," said Nakata. "I have copies. I'm not allowed back to the house, to anywhere near the estate, so I can't do any further work on them. No one can; the owners have refused all attempts to return. What I have isn't proof."

"It's enough," said Tidyman. "Proof would be nice, but it isn't about truth at this point, not completely, but about a perception of a *possible* truth."

"Yes," said Nakata, thinking, *Faith and hope, faith and hope and persuasion and other possible truths.*

"I hired you because you're very good at what you do, Mr Nakata, make no mistake, but also because you have this experience, and it may help the boy, and my job is to help the boy. A boy, Mr Nakata, at risk of losing his liberty for the rest of his life, or at least, a good portion of it, unless you can help me sow the seeds of a new truth."

"Yes," said Nakata again, helpless in the face it, the enormity of it gathering around him. Was he going to tell this, tell it all? Yes, he realised, yes he was, because it was time, and it was what Amy would want him to do. The truth can be uncomfortable in the telling, she had said to him once, and it may hurt, but it never hurts more than a lie or a silence. More often, the truth opened up new pathways, gave new opportunities to the teller and the hearer. If she were here, she'd hold his hand and smile at him and tell him to speak, that his story had to be told. If he had faith in anything, he may as well have faith in that.

"I've only ever told the police this, the police and a couple of close friends. People I trusted. I suppose I need to trust you if I'm going to tell you," said Nakata, "and if I trust you, I suppose you're among my friends. You may as well call me by my first name rather than 'Mr Nakata'."

"I'd be honoured to," said Tidyman, "if you'll tell me what it is."

"Richard," said Nakata. "My name is Richard."

"Well, Richard," said Tidyman, "tell me. Tell me about the Glasshouse Estate."

Nakata took in a long breath, held it, and then exhaled slowly, letting the tension drop from his limbs. *I have faith in you, Amy*, he thought, and then started.

"Not the whole Estate, just one house. 24 Glasshouse. One new house, in the middle of a half-finished estate. There were three of us, and we were just trying to do something that hadn't been done before. We were just taking advantage of things, trying to do. . ."

24 Glasshouse, Glasshouse Estate

"... something interesting," finished Wardle.

They had been in the car for almost half an hour now, the smell of its old and labouring engine coming in sharp exhalations of burnt oil and hot metal though the air vents. Nakata felt queasy, cramped on the rear seat between the window and piled boxes. He wouldn't have minded so much if he'd been cramped against Amy, but she was in the front passenger seat, having claimed what she called 'female privilege'.

"I still don't quite get it," said Amy.

"Richard, haven't you explained our scheme properly? A rectification immediately please: let's start at the beginning, if we can. What's a ghost?"

Amy turned in her seat and grinned at Nakata. They had spoken about this just last night, about Wardle's treatment of Nakata and why he put up with it. "You're a PhD just like him, *better* than him, he's not your boss, but you let him boss you around and I don't understand it," she had said.

"Me either," he had replied. "It's just hard to say no to him, not to fall in with what he says, that's all. Besides, he's my friend and he's not so bad. When he's on a roll, he just sort of takes you with him whether you like it or not. Whether I like it or not."

"Well," Amy had said, "we can't have that. I shall have to take you somewhere I can have you all to myself, away from his bad influence." She had laughed as she said it, but Nakata didn't think she was joking, not really. It was the first time she had ever mentioned the future in those terms and it had made him giddy to hear it. Now, he grinned back at her and said, "Of course, Mark. Now, where shall I begin your education, Amy?"

"Treat me like an idiot, a tourist," she said, still grinning that secret grin.

"An idiot? As you wish. Well, there are a number of theories as to ghosts, and I shall begin at the most obvious.

"Ghosts are the leavings of the dead. Purists and believers argue that ghosts represent some kind of remaining individual consciousness capable to some degree of independent thought and action. In this scenario, somehow a part of a person survives beyond their corporeal death. Alternatively, we might argue that ghosts have no consciousness to speak of but are, rather, images of the dead imprinted on the environment, visible or audible, occasionally tactile, but lacking will or intellect. In this scenario, seeing ghosts is like playing back a recording. This is sometimes called the 'Stone Tape' theory after a television play by the great Nigel Kneale. Lastly in this subset of theories, it has been suggested that ghosts are bundles of energy, the remains of a once-living person, but that this energy requires a human catalyst to emerge, to give it form. Once the correct catalyst is applied, the energy can come together and may have both will and intellect, but can do nothing without the initial catalyst. Poltergeists and other person-specific hauntings may fall into this category.

"Another subset of theories," said Nakata, his voice singsong. He was still grinning at Amy, who was still grinning back. He made his voice more formal, a caricature of a lecturer. "None of these first explanations is true, ghosts are merely the incorrect interpretation of stimuli. The observer sees something entirely normal but that they do not understand, and believes it to be a ghost because they have no other explanation available to them. Billowing curtains become the supernatural breath of a dead man, the noise of rats in the attic becomes footsteps of the building's previous owner, long dead and barely remembered. A variant of this may be that the interpretation is incorrect because the perception utilises skills or talents that we do not, as yet, understand; this might explain why some people experience ghosts and hauntings whilst others do not. This theory may also be regarded as a refinement of the `Stone Tape' theory, as here, there is no supernatural element, only human development as yet uncharted, with some people able to pick up on signals recorded in a way we do not yet grasp but others unable to." Nakata's singsong was peaking now, like some absurdly bubbly children's presenter explaining a complex subject.

"There are more," said Wardle, no sign of humour in his voice. "On, please!"

"There are no ghosts and no misinterpretation," continued Nakata, "all ghost stories are deliberate lies. For whatever reason, people claim to have seen ghosts but have not, in fact, seen anything. They may be after attention or profit, or be lying just for fun. They may, perhaps, feel a strange compulsion to add mystery to others' lives. Whatever the reason, it lies squarely in your domain, in the realm of the psychologists and psychiatrists and requires no further investigation from us hardworking parapsychologists." Amy grinned again; he grinned back.

"Another variant: the initial incident may belong to an earlier category or not be a ghost story at all, but is then magnified by repetition and Chinese whispers until its original cause is lost and it is assumed to have a supernatural explanation."

"Excellent," said Wardle in a 'that's done now' voice, and Nakata wanted to think he wasn't being thoughtlessly condescending and was joining in the joke, but he couldn't; he had known the man too long and Amy had, gently but firmly, pulled the last of the scales from his eyes.

"There's another explanation," Nakata said before Wardle could carry on.

"Yes?" said Wardle, sounding surprised.

"Yes," said Nakata. "That everyone who sees or hears or feels a ghost is hallucinating, and they're all fucking mad."

Amy let out a very unladylike bellow of laughter. Wardle said nothing, and for a second or two Nakata thought he'd gone too far and pushed him into a sulk; he'd done it before, although not often. Wardle drove silently for several minutes and then, as though Nakata hadn't spoken, said, "So there are several possible explanations for ghosts. Actually, there are probably hundreds of variations on those theories, but they're the main ones. Now, it's not feasible to think that everyone who reports experiencing the ghostly is lying or mistaken, and besides, cameras don't lie and we have enough photographs and film without explanation to tell us that more is going on than can be explained simply. Some ghosts appear to have cognition, others to merely repeat patterns at regular or irregular intervals. So, what's going on? That, gentleman and lady, is what we're here to find out." As he spoke, Wardle was swinging the car off the main road and down a newly surfaced lane towards something that looked like a building site.

"Welcome," he said as the car came to a halt, "to the Glasshouse Estate."

24 Glasshouse was the only house that had been completed. The others were in various stages of construction, some simply foundations and tape and poles across muddy patches of earth and others were walls without windows or with planking where the windows should be. "The financial crisis," said Wardle. "The company can't afford to carry on building because no one's buying, so they've paused until the markets pick up. We've asked if we could use the only completed building, and they've agreed."

"For a fee," said Nakata, feeling he should chip in. He had discovered Glasshouse, after all, and made most of the arrangements. The original idea had been his as well, despite how Wardle was talking; Wardle had simply hitched himself to Nakata and then charmed the department into allowing them to do this. He was good at that sort of thing, even Amy agreed. In short bursts, he could charm and persuade and argue and get his own way in a manner that Nakata hadn't yet managed to learn. It only became bullying and hectoring when he thought he'd got you under his thumb.

It took most of the afternoon to get the house ready, positioning the movie cameras and audio recorders, the thermometers and the still cameras, and then calibrating it all on the laptops set up in the kitchen. Nakata and Amy spent the last hour repeatedly walking through rooms or up and down the stairs, making sure the various devices triggered when they were supposed to and that their images and sounds were recorded clearly. By the time Wardle was satisfied with the set-up, dusk was approaching, the light deadening and the shadows beginning to thicken.

"We start tomorrow night," he said as they finally climbed in the car and started to drive away. "Tomorrow, this begins."

On paper, it sounded simple: for four weeks, they would subject an empty house to a repeated barrage of lights and sounds, and see if the house recorded any of these patterns. The day after Nakata, Amy and Wardle were at 24 Glasshouse, three of the university's theatre staff came and set up both sound and lights systems around the house, designed to repeat their programs between 6 p.m. and midnight each night. The rest of the time, the equipment installed by Nakata and Wardle was set to record any movement or noise in the house. Each morning either Nakata or Wardle, accompanied by an independent observer, went to the Glasshouse estate to check that all the equipment was working, but did not look at what, if anything, had been recorded. Neither Nakata nor Wardle knew what patterns of light and sound had been programmed to run in the house, and wouldn't until after they had been through any recordings made, which they did on the twenty ninth day.

After, they called it the Night Thirteen Recording, and without it, they probably wouldn't have carried on.

There had been false alarms during the recordings of the first twelve nights, audio recordings triggered by the car engines of the estate's security patrols, cameras coming on as the guards walked past the uncovered windows and once, both cameras and audio catching a bird hitting the lounge window and then lying twitching on the window ledge for several minutes before rolling off and disappearing from view. Nothing that could not be explained occurred until night 13.

The recording was an audio, and it started at five past one and finished at nine minutes past. Initially, it consisted simply of static that got louder and louder, but then it resolved itself into something else. "It's a fucking folk song," breathed Wardle as he and Nakata listened. Behind them, their independent observer for the day, a colleague from the English department, leaned forward and made a note on his pad.

"It is," agreed Nakata. "Is it coming from outside? From a car radio?"

"No," said Wardle, "none of the other recorders are getting anything. Look." It was true; each of the other devices in the house remained untriggered.

"One of the machines malfunctioning?"

Wardle didn't reply; the various machines around 24 Glasshouse had been checked every day, and none had malfunctioned during the first stage of the experiment. This was not an errant broadcast, a singing patrolman or a radio tuned to some obscure station, it was something in the house, in one room of the house and no more. "We have it," said Wardle as the song faded back to nothing, fiddles and mandolin dissipating into night air that was now over two weeks old. "It's there."

They checked the rest of the days quickly; there were no repetitions of the song, but other noises had been recorded on days 16 and 19, and on day 22 a voice could clearly be heard at five in the morning in the front bedroom, saying "Low, Cromarty, 982, deepening rapidly, expected German Bight 958 by 0700 tomorrow". Finally, they checked the last two recordings, taken on two random days during the experiment's 'live hours', as they called them, between six and midnight. In both, a folk song about visiting London played in the lounge, its length the exact length of the Night 13 Recording, and an old shipping forecast played repeatedly in the front bedroom.

"We did it," said Nakata. "We *did* it, with a folk song and the shipping forecast!"

"No," said Wardle. "We started it. Now, we carry it on."

There were nine people in the end, five who arrived alone and two couples. "It's simple," said Wardle. "We'll pay your expenses, and all we want you to do is to go to the house at some point between eight in the morning and midnight and do something important to you. Do it for as long or as short as you like, but do it every day, and do it in the same place within the house and for the same length of time, and be finished and gone by midnight. Read a book, ring someone, work, exercise, walk about talking, sing Gilbert and Sullivan, whatever you want. You'll need to go on record about what you've done, so bear that in mind, and don't do anything illegal, but other than that we really we don't care what you do." One of the couples looked at each other and giggled, and Nakata groaned inwardly. *They'll fuck*, he thought. *I hope to Christ they don't split up before the 28 days are over, or argue or go off each other, or that he doesn't get the droop one of the days.*

"Twenty-eight days," continued Wardle. "Four weeks of your time, that's all. Sort out between yourselves the times you'll be going to the house, use the space however you want, but please don't tell anyone what you're doing and don't take anyone with you or change your routine and don't damage anything. We start tomorrow. Questions?"

"What's this for?" asked one of group, an older student from the humanities department.

"It's for mine and Mr Nakata's PhDs," said Wardle. "If all works out, you'll help us create a ghost."

It was quicker this time. On the fourth night's recording, a figure walked the length of the hall from the kitchen to the lounge but did not show up on the other cameras, and the fifth night's audio playback contained muffled bangs and grunts coming from the upper bedroom. Two figures danced in the back bedroom on the recordings from nights 11 and 12, disappeared for three nights and then reappeared on night 16 for the last time. Something that might have been singing, unclear and tuneless, emerged during the playback of the seventh and eighth nights and lasted for over two minutes on the first night and almost a minute on the second. Despite the difference in length, both Nakata and Wardle agreed that it was the same thing being sung on both nights. The independent observer agreed.

Night 15: noises in the bathroom.

Night 20: two figures lying next to each other on the floor of the smallest bedroom, motionless but somehow animated for the entirety of their eighteen-second appearance.

Night 27: the sound of footsteps in the back bedroom, rhythmic yet shuffling, sounds that matched the movements of the dancing figures from the earlier nights.

Night 28: a figure walking across the dining room and going through the door to the kitchen but not appearing on the kitchen camera.

When Nakata and Wardle checked, under the watchful gaze of the observer, they found that everything on the recordings corresponded with the sheets the participants had completed and signed.

Dancing in the bedroom, Nakata read, *and Walking the same route through the house each night, and Singing!* The notes were followed by a list of songs, and the sheaf of paper shook in his hands. "It's incredible," he said, already starting to write the research up in his head. "We made a ghost. We made *ghosts.*"

"No," said Wardle, "we didn't, but we might have proved the Stone Tape theory. There's more, though. More we can do."

"What?" asked Nakata. "We proved it; we proved that we can imprint things in the walls and floor, in the fabric of a place. Christ, this is enough to make us famous, to get us jobs for life! We *did* it!"

"No," said Wardle again. "But we will."

"Absolutely not."

Nakata and Wardle were in the lounge of 24 Glasshouse, and for the first time that Nakata could remember, they weren't merely arguing but actually shouting at each other.

"For God's sake, Richard," said Wardle, "this is our chance! When are we going to get another opportunity like this? We've come this far, we can go further and get it all. Stone Tapes don't explain all ghosts, you know that; if we stop now, we've only shown half the picture, proved a half-truth. We've got a folk song playing out of nowhere, indistinct figures walking about the place, singing, lying next to each other, but it's *not enough.* We have to prove the next stage."

"Assuming I believe that there is a next stage," replied Nakata, his voice hard, "which I'm not sure I do, what are you suggesting, that we kill someone here, hope that they come back from the dead after and talk to us?"

"If you're going to be ridiculous, we may as well stop talking," said Wardle. "This is a big opportunity for us, the biggest we'll probably ever get, and you're being a fool. I'm not going to let you fuck it up, Richard. If you won't take the chance, fine, fuck off, I'll do it, but I'll make sure everyone knows that the most important part of this experiment, the last bit, is a solo effort. You'll be a fucking has-been, Richard. Are you ready for that?"

Was he? Nakata wondered. Was he ready to walk away from this, after they'd come so far? To let Wardle run with what had been, essentially, his idea? No, he thought, no he was not. This was his, his and Wardle's, from an idea that Nakata had been playing with for years now, ever since those first lectures and experiments with Rhine Cards, and he wasn't going to let it go now, not so close. This was his as much as Wardle's, more probably, and he was staying with it as far as they could take it. What Wardle had suggested was terrible, but it could be made to work, surely?

"Well?" asked Wardle. His face was red and he was trembling, Nakata saw.

"How would we do it?" he asked.

"You agree we should try? No backing out?" asked Wardle.

"Agree? No, but I'm not letting you do this without me. I'm in," said Nakata, "as long as we don't actually have to murder anyone." He smiled as he spoke but was alarmed to see Wardle apparently take the question seriously, a thoughtful expression dropping across his face for a moment before clearing like spent rain clouds under the glare of the sun.

"We don't have to murder anyone," said Wardle carefully, "when there are so many people prepared to die naturally. We just have to get one of them to die *here*."

It was only later, when Amy pointed it out to him, that Nakata realised just how easily he'd been manipulated, and how well Wardle had played it. Played *him*. "For God's sake, Richard," she said, "he can't run the experiment without you, it's your experiment."

"It's ours," said Nakata, defensive. They were in the tiny room that served Nakata as both study and lounge, Amy standing and Nakata seated on a sofa that he had owned for six years, and which he didn't think would last much longer. "Our experiment, I mean."

"It's not, it's always been yours; you just let him in on it. Actually, he probably made you feel like he was doing you a favour, I'll bet. He's done just what he always does, made you feel inferior to him, and there's no reason to, not one reason on earth. You're better than him, Richard, smarter and a better academic, and a nicer human being." Nakata had never seen her so angry, and was suddenly glad it was an anger aimed mostly at someone else rather than him. *Is this love?* he wondered, *Is it love when I don't want her to be this angry at me, not because I'm scared but because I don't want her to think less of me? Is that love? I think it is; I think it must be. I think I'm in love.*

In love.

"He's a user," Amy carried on, "a user, and you're letting yourself be used. Haven't you wondered why he did it when I wasn't around? He'll say it's because this is your work, I imagine, but I'll bet it's because he knows what I'd say, that you'd want to talk to me about it if I was available. Think about it, Richard, *think*! You've done enough, more than anyone has ever managed to do before, why do you need to go any further?"

"Well," said Nakata, on firmer ground now, "it's not actually a bad idea. And if we can do it, then we'll have proved something astonishing. It sounds a little odd, I grant you, but. . ."

"Odd?" interrupted Amy. "It's morbid at best, and manipulative at worst. No, at worst, it's damned *ghoulish*; is that what you want? To be remembered as Nakata and Wardle, the Burke and Hare of the ghost-hunting set?"

"That's unfair," he said, knowing it wasn't, not really. "Now you're doing what he did, trying to manipulate me, acting as though I haven't thought about the implications of this. I have, Amy, I'm not stupid."

"I know," she said, the fight suddenly gone from her, its absence deflating her so that she appeared smaller. She collapsed onto the sofa next to him. It groaned as she did so, the seat sagging as its springs stretched under their combined weight. "I know you aren't stupid and I'm sorry, but this idea, it's horrible. Can't you stop him? Think of another way to do it?"

"No," said Nakata. "Lake's arriving tomorrow."

Nakata expected someone old, but Lake was only in his mid-forties or perhaps younger; the disease made it hard to tell with any certainty. He had been bigger at some point, Nakata thought, and had lost weight as the cancer took its grip and tightened. His now-loose skin drooped, layering, forming wrinkles that had nothing to do with age and everything to do with the man's approaching death.

Lake couldn't walk, so Wardle pushed him up the path to 24 Glasshouse, wheeling him in an old wheelchair with an oxygen cylinder hanging on its back in a red nylon cradle, carrying the man's bag over his shoulder. When Nakata stepped forward and offered to take the second bag from off Lake's lap, he had his offered hand ignored; the man didn't look at Nakata except to give him a glance that lasted only the briefest of moments. Lake only really responded to Amy, giving her a smile that was presumably supposed to be open and charming but was, in fact, ghastly; it revealed dry gums that had pulled back from teeth yellowing and crooked.

"Are you my nurse? I might need a bedbath, if you are," said Lake. His voice was low and rough, as though it was being released by a dull needle dragging across years-old wax. He coughed as he finished speaking, and Nakata caught the scent of his breath; it was as though something had crawled into his lungs and died. In some ways, of course, the exact opposite had happened, Nakata thought, imagining the man's lungs gradually swelling, birthing malignant new cells as black and oily as pitch. What were they doing? Really?

"We get someone to die in 24 Glasshouse," Wardle had said, "someone angry about dying, someone who's fighting it every step of the way, and maybe, just maybe, they'll leave something behind we can see or hear or touch. That does something other than repeat patterns, that shows some sign of intelligence or personality that we can recognise, talk to, or record. If we do that, we're past Stone Tapes and into real, actual ghosts: the survival of human consciousness beyond corporeal death, Richard. Think about it. We can prove it, if only we go that step further. We can settle the argument once and for all!"

Only we can't, thought Nakata as they settled Lake for his first night in 24 Glasshouse, *not really. If we catch his ghost somehow and record it, then we'll be accused of faking it, of misinterpreting the data. And if we don't, the believers will still believe and the disbelievers will claim vindication.*

They all stayed that first night-even Amy, despite her reservations--although none of them slept, Nakata didn't think. Lake hacked and coughed most of the night, and the sound of it was dry and wrenching, interspersed with the mechanical exhalations of the oxygen canister. He spoke to Wardle sometimes, his voice low and rough, but ignored Nakata, even when Nakata asked him direct questions. He kept smiling at Amy whenever she went in the room, and once grasped her hand as she put down the drink she had brought in for him.

At about three in the morning, Amy and Nakata went for a walk, unable to listen to the man's wheezing, racketing breathing anymore. "Can't we call someone?" asked Amy once they were outside.

"No," said Nakata. "He's said no nurses, no staff, no help. He knows he's going to die, he says, and wants to do it without interference. He's sane and capable of making that choice. That's why he's here; 24 Glasshouse is a perfect place to die, according to him. I heard him tell Wardle that before." Actually, he had heard Lake say, in between wracking coughs, "If I'm going to die, better I do it here where no one's fussing about with me, although if that girl wants to fuss I wouldn't mind. I have something she can fuss with, and it still works. Give me some time with her, you go out and take your chink friend with you, and I'll show her how the dying live!" Here, Lake had deteriorated into more coughs, and Nakata hadn't waited for either Wardle's reply or for any more statements from Lake himself. He hadn't told Amy.

Outside, the night air was cold and the Glasshouse Estate was quiet. Away from 24, the other houses sat, stolid and abandoned in the darkness. Here there, diggers sat and in shadow, their backhoes curled behind them like scorpions' tails, and piles of building materials lay silent under fluttering tarpaulins. Although he couldn't hear it, Lake's cough seemed to float in the air around Nakata as he and Amy walked the estate's deserted streets. Amy put her arm around him, leaning her head against his shoulder.

"What are we going to do after this?" she asked, and Nakata didn't fail to notice the 'we'.

"I don't know," he replied. "A job, I suppose. More research. Try to lose my reputation as Burke. Or am I due to be Hare?"

"Smartarse," said Amy. "I meant us. You're almost done with your doctorate. What happens after?"

Nakata didn't reply, because he couldn't. He had always assumed he would meet someone, spend his life with them, but the actuality of it was far more complex than he had ever anticipated. Suddenly, his future was full of ghosts of things not yet real, of differing lives in which he was with Amy and married, with Amy and not married, with Amy but still working with Wardle, with Amy and a thousand miles from Wardle. The enormity of it, and the *potentiality* of it, was breathtaking. So many possibilities, so many chances for things to go right, to go wrong; how could he possibly know the best way to act? To move?

As if sensing his concerns, Amy pulled away from his shoulder but kept hold of his hand, and said, "We don't have to decide anything now, but it'd be nice to know that you're thinking about it."

"I am," he said, thinking *Once I've dealt with the death in my life, I'll deal with the life.* He thought of Wardle and a racist man dying in a house somewhere behind them. They walked on in a companionable silence, circling the whole estate of sixty plots, laid out in a series of smaller cul-de-sacs with the main road running around the outside in a large ring. The distant sound of the motorway was faded down to something like the hum of overhead power cables by distance, and the air smelled of earth and moisture and Amy's skin and the perfume she wore. The sky felt endless above Nakata, full of hope. He held Amy's hand tighter and they walked, and Nakata was happy.

"There's not enough," said Wardle to Nakata when he and Amy returned to 24 Glasshouse. He was waiting for them in the hallway, a look of concern on his face. At first Nakata thought he was talking about their ability to look after Lake, that they hadn't enough knowledge or equipment. It soon became clear, however, that Wardle was talking about something else entirely.

"He's just lying there coughing and dying."

"Isn't that enough?" asked Amy, making no effort to hide the disgust in her voice.

"No," said Wardle. "I'm worried that there's not enough of him there, that he's not putting enough of himself into the house."

"Of course," said Amy. "He's not trying hard enough. How inconsiderate of him. Perhaps he could rail against God, yes? Or do you a song and dance? Maybe make a few curses?" Stepping forward, she slapped Wardle across the face. The sound of it was loud in the hallway, sharp, followed immediately by the noise of Lake coughing again. He sounded as though his lungs were being torn to dry, ragged pieces, that he was spitting the pieces out into thick liquid and watching them sink. In the gloomy hallway, the coughing, the slap and Wardle's attitude impacted, all of them crashing together and collapsing some of the futures Nakata had seen on his walk with Amy, dwindling them until they crumpled into nothing. *A decision made for me*, he thought abstractly, stepping between the woman he loved and a man whose friendship he realised he no longer needed, if he ever truly had. "Enough," he said. "Enough."

Later, when Amy had gone upstairs, Nakata tried to talk to Wardle. Like Nakata, however, Wardle clearly realised that the slap formed a punctuation in their relationship, and he refused to look Nakata in the eye. "I'll sort this," was all he said. "You get her out of here, out of my sight. Lake doesn't want to see you anyway, so there's no point in you staying, and frankly, I don't want you here either. Once Lake's gone, we run the equipment for twenty-eight days and take it in turn to make sure it's working, as planned. Then check the recordings and after that, we can write things up separately."

"What are you going to do?"

"What you should be doing. I'll talk to Lake, get him to remember things, get him to do more than cough and die, get him to use his personality. We need him to live here and die here, not just die here, or we'll end up with the ghost that coughs and wheezes but doesn't do anything else. You go, though, and take your sensitive girlfriend with you."

Nakata didn't hear from Wardle for almost two weeks, and when he did ring, he sounded exhausted. "He's dead," he said, his voice flat and toneless.

"When?"

"Earlier today. I'll set the equipment up, make sure everything's working, and then I'm going home. I'd appreciate it if you'd do the first check tomorrow."

Nakata felt a wave of sadness, closer to nostalgia than anything active; he didn't want to recreate his relationship with Wardle, but it was hard, letting it go this way. "How was it?" he asked, wanting to extend some kind of olive branch to the man.

"How do you think? He went hard: coughing and swearing and hating everything. He stank and I stink of him and I feel like I'll never be free of the stink, but someone had to do it, didn't they? I've done nothing but talk to him, Richard, talk and listen and clean up his shit and snot and piss, and you should have been here to help, but you weren't. I hope you've had a nice time with Amy, I really do, while I've been doing our work."

What could Nakata tell him? Yes, he and Amy had had a nice time; she had, to all intents and purposes, moved in to his tiny flat, and although it wasn't official, their conversations had strayed towards marriage once or twice, and neither of them seemed to be worried by the straying. Wardle's voice sounded as though it was coming from a great distance, one measured not in miles but in the negatives of liking and tolerance and friendship. There was nothing he could do about it, he knew; there was nothing he wanted to do. "I'll be there tomorrow," he said. "I'll do the checks every day, if you like."

"Fine," said Wardle.

24 Glasshouse was quiet, but Wardle was right; it stank. In the time that Lake had been there, the smell of his flesh failing had permeated every room. It was weakest on the first floor, presumably because Lake had spent his time downstairs, but it was still there, faint and rich and spoiled. He walked around the equipment and found that it was all working fine.

Nakata was about to leave, had the door open, when he stopped. One foot outside, one foot in, and he turned. The independent verifier, another PhD student, this one from the Modern Languages department looked back at Nakata and then at his watch meaningfully. Nakata ignored him, and after a moment went back inside the house. The smell was somehow worse when it mixed with the cleaner air from outside, as though it was hiding itself, tainting the freshness with rot. He went through the house swiftly, unsure of why he'd come back in. Had he forgotten something? Some piece of equipment that he'd forgotten to check? No. Something he'd not done to or on the computer? No. No, none of that; then what? He paused in the hallway, about to open the door into the kitchen. No, not there, the dining room.

There was someone else in the house.

It wasn't a noise, nothing that Nakata had heard or seen that made him think so, but a change in how the house felt, in how its atmosphere settled about him. There was someone in the dining room, he was sure, standing quiet and listening as he listened back at them. The dining room had been empty earlier, but now there was someone in there. He went to the door, putting his head close to it but heard nothing. It was as though someone was standing on the other side of the door with their own head cocked in a mirror of his own stance.

Nakata's hand hit the handle and the rattle of it was loud in the no-longer-empty house.

He pushed down the handle, edging the door open slowly. An inch of space appeared between the door and the frame, then two and then three and there was a thing that wasn't a noise but was like the absence of noise, as if someone was tensing into complete silence, waiting behind the door, and for a second Nakata imagined them armed with a knife or an axe, holding it high and waiting.

Another inch, and the house itself seemed to take a breath, hold it. Another inch. Another.

"What are you doing?"

Nakata started, jumping about and feeling oddly guilty as he faced the PhD from Modern Languages. "I'm sorry, I thought I heard something," he said, not exactly truthfully. Turning back, he pushed open the dining room door. The feeling of expectation was gone, the tension evaporating, if it had ever been there to start with. The room was empty, although Lake's scent was stronger here, a treacle of sweat and piss and shit and something else, something fetid and dense. *Cancer*, thought Nakata as he left 24 Glasshouse. *That's the smell of his cancer, of the thing that killed him.*

Nakata thought that the smell might have started to dissipate as the week went by, but it didn't; if anything, it got stronger. He started to open the windows while he was there, partly because he wanted to breathe clean air but partly because he was growing concerned; at some point, the construction company would be back and he didn't want them chasing him or Wardle with lawsuits because they'd stunk the house out or made it unsaleable. It didn't help though; the smell remained.

On the third day, Nakata became suddenly convinced there was someone in the kitchen, peering over his shoulder as he checked the computers. It wasn't the independent observer (his PhD supervisor that day) but someone else, someone as close as they could be, fractions of an inch behind him, and although their breath wasn't tickling his ear, it was, in some way he couldn't exactly describe. When he turned around, however, there was just Dr Jones in the corner of the room, busy writing notes into the file that he and Wardle had set up at the beginning of the experiment. *Back when we were friends*, thought Nakata suddenly, and felt that wave of sadness again. He hadn't spoken to Wardle properly for, what, three weeks? Yes, apart from the brief conversation about Lake, three weeks.

There was a bang from the lounge.

Nakata looked at Jones, who looked at the door into the lounge. *At least he heard it, too*, thought Nakata, going to the lounge door. Opening it proved difficult, not because of any physical obstruction but because of that expectation again, that something he couldn't name or explain was waiting for him just beyond the painted woodwork. His hand wavered around the handle. Dr Jones was behind him, expectant in ways Nakata *could* understand, waiting, wondering what Nakata was doing. He wanted to open the door, didn't want to; something was tensing beyond it.

I can stand here forever, he thought, *or I can move forward. Get it done, get it over.* He opened the door.

The lounge was empty. Nakata and Jones looked around it carefully, peering at the shelves with their collection of bland, framed photographs and books that weren't real, and behind the stereo and television that were simply shells with no innards in the corner. The showhouse furniture was all in its place, wearing a skin of dust. "Nothing," said Dr Jones. "I was hoping that we'd open the door and find a ghost!" He laughed, stopping when he saw that Nakata wasn't joining in.

It was only as they left the room that when Nakata saw it; the imprint of a bird on the window, wings splayed wide and head turned awkwardly. It would explain the noise; they had a similar incident on film, after all, except that Nakata walked around the outside of the house, there was no bird on the ground below the window. By the time he and Jones had walked around the house to the exterior of the window, the mark on the glass itself had faded.

"It's a coincidence," said Amy later that night. "What did you tell me that day? That ghost stories are sometimes people assuming supernatural explanations for simple events? Maybe the house is just in a bad place for birds? They can't tell its there, or it's because it's new and they aren't expecting it?"

"Maybe," said Nakata, wanting to be persuaded but not.

"You left the house after an argument, in difficult circumstances; it's not hard to see why you're reactions to it are a little strained."

"Maybe," said Nakata again. It made sense. He and Wardle had already proved that the house could act as some kind of recording device, so it wasn't a surprise that he was looking for explanations that fitted into their theory. A noise was a noise, nothing more; a bird that had hit the window but not died, had immediately flown off, stunned maybe but alive. The house was just a house; the empty rooms just empty rooms.

And the smell just the smell of cancer and death.

The next day, 24 Glasshouse was quiet. It was always quiet, of course, but this was an empty silence that Nakata and his observer moved through swiftly and without incident, and it remained that way for several more days.

On the eighth day, as he went upstairs, Nakata *knew* that there was someone standing at the top of the stairs, just as he'd known that someone was behind him in the kitchen. They were around the corner, out of sight. How Nakata knew, he still couldn't say; there was no sound, no muted shuffles or breathing, no mutters of movement across the floor, but someone was there nonetheless. It was morning, and the sun was coming from the east and shining through the windows in 24 Glasshouse's upper floors, the heavy beams lancing along the hallway. Nakata took another step upwards, bringing both feet onto the next riser. The upper floor was level with his waist so that he was looking down at the varnished boards. An indistinct shadow stretched out across them, its edges stealing the sunlight and drawing it to its heart. The shadow moved, a figure waiting for Nakata away from the stairs, out of his view. The sour scent was back, not that it had ever truly been away, roiling like steam in his nostrils.

The shadow moved again, growing as though the person was suddenly approaching, causing Nakata to take a step back. His feet caught together and he stumbled, would have fallen if his observer, Dr Jones again, hadn't braced himself against his back, making a warning sound as he did so. Nakata felt the air move around him, pressing against his face and chest.

Regaining his footing was easy; calming down was harder. It was only when Jones asked, "Are you okay?" and he was forced to answer "Yes"-even though he didn't feel it- that he carried on up the stairs. Jones could, as the PhD supervisor, dismiss this experiment, and by extension a major part of his PhD, if he decided it had not been carried out correctly, so Nakata felt as though he had little choice. Bracing himself, he stepped quickly up the steps and into the hallway.

There was no one there.

There wouldn't be, of course. Nakata knew it even before he took his step, knew that the hallway would be empty and all the rooms off it deserted, just like the rooms downstairs had been that day and all the others. Why shouldn't they be? This was an unlived-in house, a show home full of fake furniture and mocked up possessions, and there was no one else here. No one.

Around his feet, Nakata watched as a shadow that had no obvious cause eddied and disintegrated.

For the next week 24 Glasshouse remained quiet. Nakata's checks were swift and uninterrupted, their equipment functioning well. At the beginning of the fourth week, he thought he heard something, or someone, walking across the bedroom but again there was no one there when he checked. The day after, he heard the sound of moving bedsprings in the dining room, but it was also empty when he opened the door. *The incidents are becoming almost commonplace*, he thought as he walked away from the room, marvelling at how easily he had gotten used to them.

The next day, he was followed around the house.

It wasn't his observer, a sallow woman called Donnelly from the administrative staff of the department, but someone else who had insinuated themselves between Nakata and Donnelly and who walked one, perhaps two, steps behind him. As before, there was nothing specific for Nakata to point to that made him feel followed, nothing he could talk to Donnelly about; there was no breath upon his neck, no touch upon his shoulder or voice in his ear, and when he looked back there was no one there except Donnelly herself, but still, there was someone with him.

Someone who hated him.

That was, possibly, the worst of it; not the person's absence or their impossible presence, but the emanations of hatred that Nakata felt, formless and sharp and somehow directed at him. Not him and Donnelly, not Donnelly at all, not the house nor anything within it except him. Just him.

He was *hated*.

There were no identifiable sounds, but there was whispering; Nakata felt it rather than heard it, a lifeless tide of air brushing past his ears without touching him, carrying with it … what? Insults? No, more than that: vitriol. It accompanied him as he walked 24 Glasshouse's hallways and rooms checking the equipment. It danced around his shoulders as he sat in the kitchen making sure the computers were still working. He wanted to ask if Donnelly heard it, but it was clear she didn't, that this was something happening in a place beyond her perception.

Sitting in the kitchen, pretending to look over the computers even though he had finished his checks, Nakata tried to focus on the feelings, to be as scientific as he could about them. *Why* did he think someone was behind him? *Why* the feeling of hate? There were no obvious stimuli: no touch on his skin or voice in his ear, nothing to see when he turned. *Nobody's* there, he told himself, knowing as he did so that he was wrong. There was someone there; he could feel it in the prickle that slipped across his skin and in the way his hair follicles tightened and pulled the hairs on his arms into uneasy attention. There was nothing he could record, nothing he could quantify, but something was there all the same, staring and hating and whispering.

There were no gaps in it, no pauses for something that he could call breath, just a constant stream of anger and hatred swirling and merging. It wasn't like whispering at all, he suddenly thought, not like someone expelling words, releasing them on a stream of exhaled air; no, it was as though words were doing the exact opposite, were dragging something together, pulling it into wholeness rather than being expelled and lost, as if they were forming a viscous black ball above his shoulders and dripping down upon him. Nakata had a sudden image of himself perched at the kitchen counter looking at the laptops as the great black mass coagulated behind him, swelling rapidly to fill the kitchen, absorbing the walls and windows, sucking down Donnelly and the chair she sat on and finally the sunlight itself, coming closer and closer to him, closer and closer and closer.

Closer. Twisting violently in his seat, he jerked away from the thing behind him and its incessant, insistent aggression, hands flying up to shield himself from attack.

There was nothing there. Sunlight spilled in through the windows, falling in elongating patches across the work surfaces and floor. Donnelly raised her head from her book and looked at Nakata, her face showing neither surprise nor annoyance. The sounds that weren't sounds continued for a moment in his ear, reaching a buzzing, shrieking crescendo before stopping. For another second or two, Nakata didn't move; the feeling of hatred had gone, the sense of something gathering behind him was gone, but 24 Glasshouse was bunched around him and he was tense before it.

Even later, when he was home with Amy, Nakata found it almost impossible to think clearly about what he had just felt, harder to explain it or rationalise it despite his wanting to. It gave him an insight then, sharper than he liked, into the difficulties that people who believed they had seen or heard or felt ghosts must feel; how to make someone believe, when you couldn't quite believe or explain it to yourself? How to avoid the curious looks, the disbelief, the accusations of fakery, lies or insanity? How could he acknowledge the existence of something whose existence he had never been sure about himself? Stone Tapes, yes; maybe even bundles of formless energy given mass and shape by human perception, but ghosts? No.

He didn't want to return to 24 Glasshouse, but he had no choice; the machines needed checking for two more days before he and Wardle could look over the recordings. And given the state of the relationship (or, more accurately, non-relationship) between him and Wardle, it had to be him. On the first of the last two visits he made a fast-paced dash through the house at a speed just short of a run. Nakata was followed by his observer, and although nothing happened, he could *feel* the something in the house. It was like being in a room where you knew there a wasp or a dangerous spider but couldn't see where it had hidden itself, where you worried about each movement in case it disturbed the creature and it lashed out. It was there, in a corner somewhere, hanging above him as he went down the hallway or crossed the room, slipping about his feet as he stood in the kitchen and checked the computers, invisible and silent and swollen, sour with venom.

The last day in the house was quiet. No ghosts, no feelings, no noises: just Nakata and his observer and the equipment, sentinel to rooms grown arid with dust and stillness. He moved through it quickly and left without looking back.

The recordings weren't empty, but neither was there anything new; there were unexplained lights, both static and moving, on three nights; another snatch of the folk song on the thirteenth night; and a voice intoning a part of the shipping forecast on both the twenty-first and twenty-third nights. It simply wasn't enough for Wardle, who went back and forward through the recordings hoping to see something that had not appeared before or hear something they had missed, but found nothing. He fell silent, sulky, angrily scrolling back and forward through the images until Nakata felt compelled to speak.

"Mark, we still did something no one ever did before," said Nakata, wondering about bridges and whether they could be built after what had happened.

"Did we?"

"Of course we did," said Nakata. "Look at it! We have lights and voices from things that aren't there, images of people lying together, walking. For Christ's sake, Mark, what is that you want?"

"More than Stone Tapes," Wardle replied. "Consciousness. Articulacy. Survival after death." He sounded sad as he spoke, disappointed. Nakata didn't reply; the gulf between them was greater than he knew how to cross. He wanted to mention his feelings at the house, although he had no evidence for them, nothing scientific that they could use, but he didn't. They were confidences he wasn't prepared to include Wardle in, not anymore. The two of them went their separate ways and didn't speak again except via email, and then only formally, until the construction company got in touch.

The men won't go in the house anymore, the man on the phone had said, once he calmed down, *what did you do?* He had said more, lots more, most of it vacillating between angry and confused, threats and questions. The company would sue them, he said, they'd ruin them, expose them, and although Wardle and Nakata agreed that it was probably bluster, they had to respond somehow.

24 Glasshouse didn't look any different; it was just a house, sitting amongst other houses in the centre of a new estate, noisy with the sounds of motors and shouts and hammering. The air smelled of diesel and exhaust fumes, and the sleeping mechanical lizards were awake and moving, their battered yellow-and-orange paintwork bright in the sun. Wardle was already inside 24 Glasshouse, passing occasionally across one of the windows as he walked around the building. Nakata was outside watching for him, trying to see from his stance and movements what was happening.

Nakata didn't want to go inside.

The journey had been strained, uncomfortable. Wardle and Nakata had spoken politely to each other, but that was all. When Nakata had tried to take the conversation forwards, to be friendly, and asked how Wardle was doing, Wardle had closed Nakata down with a brusque "None of your business; we'll get the house sorted and that's it."

Get the house sorted. How were they going to do that, Nakata wondered as Wardle appeared in its doorway and waved him in. How were they going to sort this? Ask Lake, assuming it was him, to leave? Exorcise his spirit? Knock up a ghost-killing machine, run it in 24 Glasshouse until the house was clear? Ignore it, hope it wasn't real or that it would fade with time?

"Come on," said Wardle. "What are you waiting for?"

Nakata didn't move, thinking about voices that weren't voices and things that weren't there when he looked. Wardle came out of the house, walking along its short path to where Nakata stood, and asked, "Well?" and then, immediately on its heels, "Christ, did you know?"

"No," said Nakata, knowing that Wardle would see the lie; Nakata was a bad liar, and Wardle was good at seeing people's weaknesses and exploiting them.

"How did you know?" asked Wardle, gripping Nakata's arm tightly. "How? These idiots are threatening to sue us, Richard, so anything you know has to help."

Nakata glanced at the windows of 24 Glasshouse again, seeing behind their panes a pulsating, vitriolic darkness, glimmering and raging, and said, "I felt it too."

"Felt what?"

"Lake, I presume. Something in the house, anyway, something angry and unpleasant."

"Richard, for fuck's sake, why didn't you tell me?"

"Because there's nothing to tell, because there's no evidence," replied Nakata, and felt shame. He *should* have told Wardle, even though there was no way they could write it into their reports. "It was subjective," he continued, "just my feelings, sensations, thoughts. I felt something, heard something, but I can't really explain what."

"Try," Wardle said, his voice a low hiss. "Try fucking hard, Richard, and try now, inside the house. Explain all this to me, Richard, explain how you can decide not to tell me. Now, Richard, please, I'm keen to fucking know."

Nakata told Wardle as they walked around 24 Glasshouse, pacing its hallways and rooms, ending up in the kitchen. Their equipment was gone now, and the room felt oddly empty.

"It didn't like you?" asked Wardle when Nakata had finished.

"More than that, it *hated* me," said Nakata, "the way someone might hate a bug or a stain on their carpet, like I was below consideration, that my very existence was offensive."

"That makes sense," said Wardle.

"Does it? Why?"

"Because Lake was a racist shit," said Wardle. "I realised when I spent all that time with him. He kept talking about 'Jews' and 'niggers' and 'chinks', kept blaming them for his illness, although how he made that little connection I have no idea. If it's Lake, then it would hate."

"We made a racist ghost?" asked Nakata. "And you didn't know that this might happen, that it's what Lake was like?"

"No," said Wardle, "how could I?"

"By doing some research," said Nakata, suddenly furious. "By checking instead of leaping forwards without fucking considering. By actually thinking about what you're doing! Christ, Mark, how hard can it have been to find out more about the man? But no, you have a grand plan, and suddenly we're stuck with a house that makes people uncomfortable, that hates anyone who's not white, and you know the worst of it? We can't prove anything, so it was all in fucking vain anyway!"

Wardle didn't reply. Nakata wanted to take his silence as some kind of acknowledgement, but knew that it wasn't; the expression on the man's face was stony, set in a defensive rictus that he knew well. Wardle had been criticised. Wardle didn't like the criticism. Wardle was right and everyone else was wrong.

Eventually, they had to talk again, although Wardle's voice was flat and chill. Nakata suspected his own was the same.

"If we can't prove anything, neither can the company," said Wardle. "They've got nothing on us. We can walk away and tell them to fuck off."

"No," said Nakata. "We know there's something here; it's not about proof."

"I thought you said you were a scientist," said Wardle. "Proof's what we need most of all."

"We're not leaving it like this," said Nakata. "This is our doing, so we need to sort it out, undo it."

"We can't undo it," said Wardle. "We gave him an empty house, filled it with his personality. That's what we were trying to do. It's a shame we can't prove anything, but it's not our responsibility. He had to die somewhere, that's the point, isn't it?"

"Is it? I wonder," replied Nakata, thinking *We gave him a blank canvas and asked him to draw, to paint, whatever. So, now his is the only image there? No, no it's not because we still recorded the things from before Lake. It wasn't a blank canvas, not completely, there were small things there already, things we put there before we let Lake in. So, can we record over him? We can't delete him, not exactly, but can we drown him out, replace him with something that doesn't hate? We can. We can, I think we can. I think.*

"What?" asked Wardle.

"I have an idea," said Nakata. "I have no idea whether it'll work, but it might. It might. I have to ring Amy."

"Why are we here?"

Amy looked up at 24 Glasshouse. The sun caught in its windows and shivered out at them, cataracting the panes so that the inside of the house became murky. Around them, the sound of construction made the air throb.

"Do you trust me?" said Nakata.

"Yes."

"Then trust me now. This isn't how I wanted this to happen, but there's a reason. Come with me." He led her into the house, the box in his pocket digging its edges into him. For the first time in his relationship with her, Nakata was keeping something secret from Amy and the weight of it was surprisingly heavy.

"Hello, Amy," said Wardle as they entered the building. Nakata shot him a look that Wardle returned, his eyes like water-slick slate. They had argued over his presence, neither backing down. The eventual compromise was that he would remain in the kitchen while Nakata and Amy walked around the house and talked.

"Hello, Mark," said Amy, glancing at Nakata. Nakata nodded, pushing her gently on, past Wardle, past the kitchen doorway and into the lounge. This was where Lake had spent the most time, coughing and hating and dying and raging, and his smell was in here still. His hate was in here, too; Nakata could feel it, like a vast and mazy glaring eye peering down at him from above. There was something else, as well, a sense of salacious interest directed at Amy. She felt it, too, he thought, as she stepped closer to him, wrapping an arm around his waist.

"You know what we tried to do here? What we did?"

"Yes," said Amy. She knew it all, and Nakata knew she did. His question was just padding, baffles between him and where he needed, *wanted*, to go next.

"So I have to do this here, but I would have done it anyway, Amy. I need you to understand that."

"Okay," she said, looking up at him. Nakata thought she had never been so beautiful, her face smooth, her lips parted slightly, her hair falling back from her forehead in tumbles that curled around her shoulders. He felt the press of her breasts against him, the weight and warmth of her arm around him, and wanted to keep the feeling forever. He reached into his inside pocket and removed the letter, holding it up so that she could see it.

"What's that?"

"The future," he said. "Ours, hopefully. It's a job offer."

It had come earlier in the week, a lectureship dependent on him attaining his PhD. He hadn't told Amy because the offer had made him think about what he did next, what he wanted to do and where Amy fitted in it. The first part of his secret, leading on to his second. "I love you," he said, "and I want to take the job. Will you come with me?"

"Yes."

"Don't you want to know where the job is?"

"No. You'll be there, so I'll be there, that's all that matters."

Such faith, Nakata thought, almost overwhelmed by it. She trusted him enough to follow him and enough to know that they'd be okay if they were together. He felt a wave of love, helpless and huge and wonderful, and said, "But there's a problem."

He felt her tense and grinned at her. Letting the letter drop to the floor, he reached down into his trouser pocket. For a moment his hand was caught between her flesh and his, and then he had the box and took it out. "I couldn't work out how to do this," he said. "I would have asked you this somewhere else, but then I thought that it didn't matter, not really. Here's as a good a place as any, better really, if it helps get rid of Lake. Amy, will you marry me?"

The ring was tiny, the stone a fleck of diamond, glittering as Nakata opened the box like a piece of captured daylight.

"Richard?" Amy breathed, and then, "Yes. Yes. I love you. Yes."

It was the happiest Nakata had ever been, and it was what he'd hoped and what he wanted. *We have to fill the place with happiness*, he'd told Wardle, *drive Lake out by overwriting him with something positive: make this place good. I know how to do it, if it works.* And it was working, he thought. They were happy, so happy, both of them and they were holding each other and Nakata was slipping the ring onto her finger and the future was unfolding before them like the wrappings of some precious gift, and he kissed her.

The room screamed.

Nakata had almost forgotten where they were, why he had asked Amy here, but the scream reminded him. It was terrible, the yowl of something pained and furious and spitting. Amy shrieked and raised her hands to her ears, but Nakata took hold of her wrists and pulled the hands away. "Amy," he said, "try not to be frightened, try to remember I love you. Do you love me, Amy?"

"Yes," she said, and their love was there in the room, greater than hate could ever be, soaking into the walls, loosing anger from the bricks and wood in chunks, like pieces of torn flesh. There was a huge boom and the house shook, its walls jittering as Lake, what was left of Lake, was torn loose from the building and then crashed back into it and tried to keep hold. Nakata couldn't see what was happening but knew it instinctively, could feel the battle going on around him.

"We'll get married," he said, trying to keep his voice conversational. "Find a house, maybe have children or not, we can decide that later. We'll be together, you and me, far from here, together."

"Yes," Amy said again as the room screamed and another huge crash sounded. She was crying now, tears spilling down her cheeks. "Please, take me home, Richard. Please."

"Yes," he said, and the room screamed for a third time, the *house* screamed, a wordless howl with bitterness and hate nestled at its heart. It echoed every foul word that had ever been hurled at Nakata, every insult about his skin or his eyes or his parents, of his mixed-race heritage. It smelled of beer and spittle and cigarettes and unwashed skin and intolerance and burning, selfish rage, and he could almost see it, tarlike, dripping out of the walls.

The house screamed again; no, not the house, someone else. Someone in the house, someone without a lover to hold onto against the shrieking unpleasantness: someone alone and brittle with arrogance and self-interest.

Wardle. Jesus, *Wardle!*

Nakata went to the hallway, pulling Amy with him. The kitchen door banged open and then crashed shut again, revealing Wardle for a moment. He was bent backwards over the breakfast counter, and he was swarming with shadows. Amy screamed, a high counterpoint to the house's bass bellow, and the door flew open again, showing Wardle battering around with flailing hands and trying to push himself backwards across the counter. Nakata took an unsteady step forward, but the door smashed shut again and the house screamed, lower, wailing. Amy gripped his arm and pulled him, their roles reversing, saying "Let's go, Richard, please, let's go."

"No," he said, thinking *It's Lake, he's losing his grip, so he's attacking the only thing he can, Wardle--who's selfish and angry and convinced of his own rightness. Attacking everything that Lake represented, all of his own weaknesses. We almost have him, we're so close.* Nakata turned to Amy and took her in his arms, saying, "Trust me," and kissed her. Around them, the house screamed again and Nakata had the impression that the walls were weeping, the drips falling upwards and collecting above them, hovering over them. He carried on kissing Amy, tasting her, loving her, breathing her in and breathing himself out.

Above them, from somewhere in one of the bedrooms, a snatch of song suddenly blared forth; Nakata recognised it as one of the folk songs that had been sung in 24 Glasshouse during the second part of their experiment. Lights flickered and a shadow in the vague shape of a person moved past them, crossing the hallway before dissolving to nothing. *Lake's taking everything else with him as he goes*, thought Nakata, *clinging to it and ripping it loose.* He didn't know how he knew it, but he did, instinctively and absolutely. This was Lake tearing at whatever reality he now knew, screaming and tearing and being torn. Amy broke their kiss as more huge crashes shook the house, pulling him towards the door, and this time Nakata allowed himself to be pulled. Her face was twisted, fearful, and he wanted her out of there and safe. Their escape was as much about love as the kiss was, their love was keeping them moving, and it was poured out of them and washed across the walls. Lake, the pieces of Lake, his hatred and anger, swilled above them. Nakata felt it staring down, hating him for his genes, for his history and for the history Lake assumed him to have, for his relationship with Amy. For his *life*.

The kitchen door opened again and this time Wardle staggered out, still flapping at the air as though he was being attacked by bees and was trying to ward them off. Nakata went to grab him, but Wardle swerved out of range, throwing a wild punch towards Nakata that connected hard with his temple and sent him staggering sideways into the wall.

"Mark, come on, we have to get out," Amy shouted as black shadows coalesced in the air around Wardle's head, seeming one moment to be hands and then the next teeth and then hands again, gripping and grasping and desperate. Nakata didn't know if they were actually there or if he was imagining them. His vision swayed as he tried to stand straight, his legs weak. Amy let go of him and went after Wardle.

The scream sounded again, less angry now, more desperate, terror mingling with the fury. Another shadow figure walked past them and then dissolved: another piece of the experiment gone. An announcer's voice echoed briefly from upstairs before fading, and then Wardle was at the stairs and climbing, and Amy was close behind him.

Nakata tried to follow them, but as he came away from the wall the world wavered around him, tones of grey and black shifting at the edges of his vision. Wardle's punch must have caught him badly; he felt as though he was horizontal, that the world had tilted on its side, and he fell to his knees. Looking up was like looking into a kaleidoscope barrel, contorted and shifting.

Wardle was at the top of the stairs, still thrashing his arms around, shrieking. Pieces of Lake remained, clinging to Wardle, shredding, dripping away, and Nakata had time to think, *We've done it, he's gone*, and then Amy was with Wardle, turning him, trying to get him to come down the stairs. Wardle screamed again.

As Amy turned him, Wardle saw her and shouted something unintelligible. Later, Nakata was never able to work out what he'd said, not even with the benefit of hindsight and context and hours of going over and over it. He wanted to think that Wardle was hysterical, that he hadn't seen Amy, had seen some other piece of Lake still grappling at him, but he wondered; in his darkest hours, he wondered. Wardle reached out and grasped at Amy, tripping, tumbling into her, pushing her back so that they both staggered, tilted, overbalanced.

Fell.

The house shrieked for nearly the last time, a whirling cry of triumph. Nakata shrieked, willing his legs to work but unable to rise. Amy shrieked, a wail of panic and pain; even Wardle shouted as he and Amy fell. The loudest sound of all, however, louder than anything else, louder than any noise in the world before it or since, was the dry *crack* of Amy's neck breaking as she hit the lowest riser.

Seconds later, Wardle's head banged against the same riser and there was another dull crunch. Blood sprayed from his mouth in a ragged fan, darker than the shadows that fluttered around his head. He rolled over like a disorganised gymnast and collapsed, fully sprawled in the hallway.

Nakata crawled, not trusting his legs, reaching out to Amy. Her head lolled towards him, her mouth open and slack. He wanted to touch her, wanted to lift her and hold her, but dared not. A thin string of blood rolled out from the corner of one eye and she blinked; one eye closed and opened more slowly than the other. "Amy," Nakata said, and the house screamed again, a last howl that tore against Nakata as Lake was finally shredded to nothing. Lights danced around Amy's head, catching in Nakata's eyes.

"I love you," he said, "please don't leave me." More lights drifted from her mouth as he spoke, coloured sparks that glinted, the reflections drifting across her eyes. They twisted around each other in the air between them, expanding like bubbles rising through water and began to float upwards. Wardle made a sound, a moist gurgle, and Nakata looked briefly over at him. Blood was pouring from the man's ears, pooling beneath his head. Nakata turned back to Amy.

She was smiling at him, or trying to; her mouth was curled up at the corners, her lips red with bloodied saliva. "Amy, I love you," he said again, and she breathed out a string of sounds that he wanted to believe were the words "I love you, too". More lights emerged, a last colourful surge, jigging around her, rising from her mouth, from her head, floating up and settling against the walls. Nakata watched as they settled, glimmering, and then burst like soap bubbles. He looked back to Amy, but what lights had been around her and in her were gone. Her eyes had rolled back, showing bloodshot sclera and her mouth sagged more widely open.

"I love you," Nakata said. He shifted, turning himself to sit alongside her and raised her head into his lap. Moving her no longer mattered. He looked up; from where Amy's lights had hit the walls and ceilings, patches of brightness were spreading. The house, Lake, moaned and the noise was spineless and shallow. Nakata stroked Amy's hair, wondering how he should feel. Sad? Angry? Hopeful that Lake had gone, that they had been successful? He thought that they had; the house felt different since the last noise, he could feel it even through his confusion and fear and grief. He and Amy had loved each other in 24 Glasshouse, had made the beginnings of a promise to share their future, and it had been enough to unseat Lake, and the past, from the building.

Wardle made another noise, a liquid rattle, as a second spray of blood came from his mouth and joined the widening stain on the floor. Lights came from his mouth with the spray, smaller and less bright than had emerged from Amy, fluttering across Nakata's vision like fireflies. They rose briefly, vanishing before they reached the walls or ceiling. Nakata knew without needing to check that Wardle was dead; the lights had told him. Even Wardle helped get rid of Lake, Nakata thought, acting like some sacrificial lamb, drawing him out in some way that he couldn't understand. Kinship? Possession? Desperation? Nakata didn't know, didn't care.

24 Glasshouse eased itself around the new emotions seeding its walls and the dead flesh cooling in its hallway. It was quiet, calm. Nothing hovered in its air; nothing glared or hated or slipped behind Nakata and peered over his shoulder, watching him. Whatever had been here, it was gone. Amy was gone. Wardle was gone. Lake was gone. Nakata stroked Amy's hair, and suddenly knew how he felt.

He hurt.

Nakata 7: Curtin's Office

"This is ridiculous," said Solomon. "You're seriously trying to claim that ghosts made your client act the way he did?"

"No," said Tidyman, leaning back in the chair and looking for all the world as though he was discussing life's inconsequentialities after a good meal rather than the technicalities of a court case. "I don't believe we've ever mentioned ghosts, have we, Richard?"

"No," said Nakata. He had been very careful in writing the various cases up, cautious about the words he used and the way in which he expressed himself. "This isn't about ghosts."

"No?" said Solomon, his voice wet with sarcasm and anger. "Then what is it about?"

"That," said Judge Curtin, "is a valid question. Mr Tidyman, Mr Nakata, I still am a little unsure as to the point of this request."

They were in Curtin's office. Nakata had expected lots of old, dark wood, walls lined with legal tomes, sombre shadows gathering in the corner, perhaps a picture of Curtin in his robes on the wall, but in actual fact it was brightly lit and modern. Curtin's robes were on a hangar on the back of the door and his wig was on a wooden, faceless head on a shelf behind him. In one corner was a small wheeled suitcase, open and half-full of books.

"We merely wish to illustrate a key element of my client's defence," said Tidyman.

"This is ridiculous," repeated Solomon. "You client's defence is that he saw something that frightened him, leading him to compound the illegal act he was already engaged in with another, more serious, illegal act. Namely, murder."

"My client has never denied what he did, only the reasons behind it," said Tidyman. "His statement, given at the time, and all statements given since are entirely consistent with each other. I simply hope to illustrate certain elements of those statements."

"Thank you both," said Curtin. "I am aware of the facts of this case. What I am a little confused about is Mr Nakata's role here."

"Oh, Mr Tidyman wishes to use Mr Nakata as his defence. He intends to show, using guesswork and fringe sciences, that the building itself somehow affected the defendant, made him act the way he did," said Solomon, openly contemptuous. When he spoke again, he affected a hollow, booming tone. "Unquiet houses, where evil lurks!"

Nakata, feeling like the tennis ball in some complex legal match, said, "No."

"Pardon, Mr Nakata?"

"It is not an untested science, nor a fringe one. There are many examples of it being an accurate science, or of science or society choosing to ignore it; the psychic Eileen Garratt passed information to the R101 airship disaster enquiry, given to her via mediumistic messages, which was never discussed as it was based on what the chairman considered 'unproven material'. Recent investigations have shown that her visions of the disaster's cause were entirely accurate. *The Journal of Personality and Social Psychology* recently published a study that appears to prove pre-sentience, and *New Scientist* has recently stressed the importance of studying these subjects scientifically, without prejudice.

"As to it being an 'unquiet house', that's also not true. My research clearly indicates that the places where these feelings occur, where people experience these things, are *quiet* houses, places where the din of the world recedes and allows other things to be heard. This isn't about ghosts or ghouls or demons any more than it's about telepathy or psychokinesis or psychosis; it's about *places*. There are places that hold feelings, hold memories, hold sights and sounds, in ways we don't understand, that can be read in certain circumstances by certain people."

"And our contention is that my client had one of those experiences," said Tidyman. "Nothing more, nothing less."

"Indeed," said Curtin. "And you propose to show this how, precisely?"

"By doing an experiment with the jury," said Nakata. *Scientific*, he told himself. *Scientific and professional.* "We take them to the site of the incident and to two other similar places, under similar conditions. We let them *experience* the places, ask them to record their sensations and feelings and perceptions, look for similarities across the recordings. We try to show how some places, *quiet* places, can have resonances that can be read and felt."

"For God's sake," said Solomon, "this is preposterous. Your honour, are you really going to let this nonsense stand?"

For a moment, Curtin didn't speak but simply looked at the three of them. He glanced at the reports on his desk, the folders with Nakata's dry write-ups, photographs, news clippings and photocopies, and then focused on Nakata. "It is an unusual request," he said, "and I can see a thousand ways in which this might adversely affect the trial and lay the court open to accusations of, at best, incompetence and at worst gross idiocy. However, your reputation in the field is impressive, Mr Nakata."

"Thank you."

"Don't thank me for the facts, thank me instead for what I'm about to do. I am minded, Mr Nakata, to take a leap of faith here, to allow Mr Tidyman to present you as a defence expert and to allow you to run your experiment."

"For Christ's sake!" said Solomon.

"No," said Curtin, "for Justice's sake, and Mr Solomon, you will keep a civil tongue in your head whilst in my office. I will be honest and state that I don't believe that this line of defence will achieve anything, but I will let it go ahead because, if there is even the slightest chance that there is some truth in it, then it deserves to be heard."

"I must protest, in the strongest possible terms," said Solomon.

"Noted," said Curtin, "and overruled. Do your experiment, Mr Nakata. Find your proof, if it exists."

"I will, thank you," said Nakata, thinking about Curtin's phrase 'a leap of faith'. He thought about Amy again, about Wardle bleeding, about footsteps in the grass and missing children and cold spots in lavatories and art that moved. *A leap*, he thought, *a leap with an unsure landing*. He rose, nodding at Tidyman and Curtin, meeting Solomon's eye briefly. *Time to go*, he thought, *time to jump.*

Stack's Farm, Trough of Bowland

The track was bumpy, jolting Nakata and the jurors. Solomon, driving, swore quietly as they went over each rut, the pig's-grunt grind of the suspension and his voice merging. Tidyman, in the front passenger seat, made no sound, his eyes closed and his hands folded across his lap.

They jolted to a halt on a muddy expanse in front of the main house. It was a squat building, two storied with small windows and a grey slate roof. Large barns stood at either side of the house, a mix of older and newer constructions. Large lights had been set up at each corner of the space in front of the house, the arcs of their brightness cutting through the night. They would be turned off when the jurors were out of the car.

"You all know what you're doing?" asked Nakata. The jurors nodded, stretched. Several yawned; it was almost two in the morning. "You have your pads? Pencils?" More nods, another yawn. One of them made a joke about having a glamorous night out at the government's expense, one or two of them laughed half-heartedly.

"Go everywhere, with others or alone," reminded Nakata. "Use your torches to see, explore as much as you can. Please don't talk to each other about what you see or feel or hear, simply record any feelings or sensations you experience in each place you go, anything you see or hear. Was it cold? Warm? Did you hear an owl? Is there a particular smell? Anything and everything, please." Nods, one or two grumbles. There was nothing more he could say to them; they knew this anyway, having visited two other farms over the previous two nights. The two earlier ones were the experiment's controls, designed to pick up the sensations in 'normal' places although under the same circumstances. The order of the farm visits was randomised, and it was only luck that they were visiting Stack's Farm on the last night of the experiment. The jurors didn't know that this was Stack's Farm, that this was where the murder had occurred.

Once the jurors had dispersed, some going into the house and some towards the outbuildings, Nakata turned the exterior lights off. The moon was high but hidden by clouds so that its light was hazy and diffuse, and the shadows pooled thickly across the rutted ground. The three men sat in the van, silent. It was a warm night, muggy, and they left the doors open. Cows lowed in one of the sheds, their feet stamping muted tattoos on the concrete floor. Somewhere distant, a bird hooted; Nakata had no idea what kind.

"Do you really think this is worth the time?" asked Solomon suddenly. He had insisted on being here, refusing to allow the experiment to go ahead without what he called 'independent representation'. Nakata agreed happily; an independent observer, or even better, a disbelieving one, would make a more powerful witness if anything happened. At the very least, they would provide strong evidence that the experiment was not flawed, and prevent accusations of cheating. This was the first time the man had spoken other than to confirm practical details or answer direct questions.

"I don't see why not," said Nakata. "The likelihood is that one or more of the jury will be receptive to any influence this place has. If we can show that they had the same kind of responses and feelings that Mr Tidyman's client had, we can show that he's telling the truth."

"'Mr Tidyman's client'," repeated Solomon. "Don't you know his name?"

"No," said Nakata, "and I don't want to. It doesn't matter, and the less I know the better; that way I can't be accused of somehow influencing the jury's findings. How can I unduly influence them, if I don't know the details myself?"

"You haven't read his statement?"

"Mr Nakata hasn't read any of the case files," said Tidyman. "He will be allowed to view them only when the jurors' notes from this experiment are completed and handed over, and only the relevant portions then. The aim of this isn't to prove anything other than the possibility that my client is telling the truth and that he did feel what he says he felt, see what he says he saw and hear what he says he heard."

"He's manipulating you," said Solomon. "It's obvious."

"Is it?" said Tidyman. "Well, maybe so. I have been appointed to provide his defence, however. He has made a statement regarding his experiences on the night of the incident, which he has consistently stuck to, and as his lawyer I have to use these statements and any corroborating evidence I can find to present the best defence I can. I believe what we are doing here to be a relevant course of action in pursuit of investigating-and possibly verifying-my client's statements and potential corroborating evidence, and thus his defence." Their pointed formality was prickling the air in the vehicle, making it like sitting in a nettle-bed, and Nakata swung his legs out and stood. The atmosphere smelled of mud and silage and grass and diesel. Solomon also climbed out of the van.

"There's no science to this," he said, coming around the front of the vehicle.

"There is," said Nakata, "just as much as there is in psychology or sociology. The experiments we carry out are done under the most rigorous scientific conditions, in the laboratory whenever possible, have been from Rhine onwards. Most of the time we're actually studying people's reactions rather than the causes of their reactions, in the hope of gaining understanding about how those reactions are generated. What are the forces at work? How do people read those forces? It's a question of generation and recording."

"Mumbo jumbo," said Solomon. He was a flat-earther, Nakata knew, locked up against the possibility of anything except the orthodoxy. *Four hundred years ago, he'd have been burning me at the stake,* he thought, *or denying the existence of meteors. One hundred years ago, he'd have been one of the people claiming that a shark's jaws weren't strong enough to injure a human swimmer. I wonder how long something has to be accepted by the mainstream before he believes it?* To change the subject, he asked, "What happened to the farm after the murder?"

"Until the verdict, whatever it happens to be, it's a crime scene, and so nothing can be done with it. It's not active as a farm anymore, though. The livestock was sold or slaughtered," said Tidyman, also exiting the car and coming around to where Nakata and Solomon were talking, "and the money was put into the estate. Eventually, I suppose, the family will have to decide whether to sell up or carry on."

"There's no livestock?" asked Nakata.

"No," said Tidyman.

"Then why can I hear cows?"

The three of them looked towards the nearest barn. Two jurors had gone in there before, Nakata remembered, and the large door was now open a few feet. The sound of cows lowing was louder than earlier, riding a rhythm of hoof-falls and the metallic tutting of the animals bumping into the walls of the enclosures.

"They were sold," Solomon confirmed.

"Another farmer? Using the barns to house his cattle?" asked Nakata.

"No," said Solomon. "It's a crime scene. The only people with permission to be here are us."

"I can't hear anything," said Tidyman, a hint of irritation in his voice. "What are you talking about?"

"You can hear it?" asked Nakata.

"Yes," said Solomon. "Cows. In the barn."

There was a noise, a low, solid thump followed by a liquid swish. One cow mooed loudly; others joined it. The sound of their movement, the rattle of stall bars and gates, became louder, more agitated. Another thump and swish, and then another, cutting a cow's ragged grunting off. Solomon looked at Nakata, and then at Tidyman, who shrugged. "I can't hear anything," he said.

"There are jurors in there," said Nakata, and started walking to the barn. "We could see if they can hear them as well."

"No," said Solomon quickly. "You don't speak to them about that, those are the rules, Mr Nakata."

"Yes," Nakata replied, thinking, *He has his faith, his belief in the rule of law, and we are not allowed to threaten that. It's fair, I suppose.*

At the barn door, the noises were louder and they were accompanied by a smell; a stench, really, of cow shit, old and rotten and cold. Nakata looked about; Stack's Farm was old but clean, partially modernised, if the buildings were anything to go by, yet this smelled unclean, unwashed and musty.

Another thump, followed by a tremble through the earth as though something heavy had slammed down into it. Another, and another tremble. More moos, hoarse and loud, and more bumps and heavy steps as the cows shifted in their stalls. Metal rattled, the sound of chains swinging, the atonal rasp of something heavy being dragged across concrete.

"We have to go in," said Nakata.

"No," said Solomon. "We call the police and let them sort it out." He took out his mobile phone, dialling and holding it to his ear.

"Really, what are you two talking about?" said Tidyman, coming up behind them.

"You can't hear them?" said Solomon.

"Hear what?" asked Tidyman again. Nakata looked back across the drab farmyard, waiting for Solomon to make his call. Torchlight played across the inside of the house windows, jurors investigating. In the top windows, two or three beams merged, create a bright square across which shadows slipped and stretched.

"Jesus! What's that?" Solomon asked. The phone dropped away from his ear, the faint digital noise of an unconnected call coming from it like the call of distant seabirds.

"I don't know," said Nakata. A tall figure was emerging from the house doorway, stooping to get its head under the frame. Its skin looked mottled, as though mould were growing across it in large, dark patches.

"It was skinny." said Solomon quietly, "'and tall'. He said that." Nakata didn't ask who had said it. Tidyman was frowning, a look of confusion crossing his face. More lights danced inside the windows, shadows bleeding around their coronas, the glass yellowing and patched like old sepia. The figure straightened, stepped forward into the shadows near the cars, its edges fraying as it went, seeming to fade away into the darkness.

"What the fuck was that?" said Solomon. "What the fuck is this?"

"What the fuck was *what*?" said Tidyman. "Richard, what's going on?"

"I don't know," said Nakata.

Someone in the house screamed.

Tidyman, the slowest of the three, went across to turn on the external lights as Solomon and Nakata ran towards the house. There was a second scream, this one less urgent, more like the burning of excess fear than any-thing active, and then they were at the door. It swayed, half open, the house's dark maw appearing and disappearing as it moved.

Behind them, Tidyman activated the lamps, spars of light stuttering at first and then filling the space around them. Their shadows leapt ahead of them, spraying across the farmhouse walls, elongated and mute. Nakata's shadow lay across the entrance, and for a moment it looked as though he was emerg-ing from it rather than moving towards it, spreading out from the house like an inky stain.

"There's no light inside," said Solomon, breathing hard.

"The jurors have torches," said Nakata, "and light from outside should get in through the windows." A third scream sounded, this one low and mis-erable. As the two men reached the doorway, a figure appeared. Nakata's breath caught until he realised that it was a normal-sized, stocky man holding a torch, his face red and his eyes wide.

"What's happening?" the man asked.

"We don't know, but I'm sure it's nothing," said Solomon, his voice smooth. Nakata watched as the lawyer's carapace came up as easily as pulling on a shirt, becoming professional, placing a reassuring hand on the man's arm and with the other gently taking the torch from him. "Go to the van, please, and Mr Tidyman will make sure that you're comfortable. I think he has coffee in flasks."

They made sure that the man was with Tidyman before entering the farm. Solomon flicked on the torch, showing a large hallway, its only furniture a phone on a small table. The phone handset was off its base unit, lying on its side, a red LED flashing at them monotonously. Seeing it seemed to remind Solomon of his own phone, which he took from his pocket and raised to his ear again. "No signal," he said. "Is that normal for this kind of situation?"

"What kind of situation?" asked Nakata.

"You know," Solomon replied, "this sort of thing. Ghosts."

"What ghosts?" said Nakata. "We haven't seen anything or heard anything that we can say is a ghost; we've just experienced things we can't yet explain. We're in a farm in the middle of nowhere; your phone provider may not have coverage here. That's precisely my point about this place, and the places like it; we react differently because the stimuli are different, less easily explain-able." As he spoke, he picked up the handset from the table and put it to his ear: no signal.

"Don't lecture me," snapped Solomon. They had come to the end of the hallway, where a doorway led into the kitchen. Solomon shone his light into the room, picking up two figures seated at the large wooden table.

"Hello?" he said. Neither figure moved.

Solomon went into the kitchen; Nakata followed. He reached out and flicked the wall switch, trying to turn the lights on, but they remained dark.

"There's no power," said Solomon. "It was disconnected. The lights outside are run on batteries brought in for the occasion. This little experiment of Tidyman and yours is costing a fortune." The professional carapace was bringing the flat-earther back, Nakata realised.

Solomon's torch beam leapt across the kitchen. It showed a large room, dust hanging in the air, a table at its centre. The light caught in the table's scarred wooden surface, its gullied grip drawing the illumination to it in pooled shadows. The reflected light washed up the walls and the cupboards that lined it, glimmering across the face of the cooker and refrigerator. The kitchen was far more modern than Nakata had expected, the electrical equipment recently updated, the work surfaces gleaming under their skin of dust. The couple sitting at the table were both female, Nakata saw: an older woman who he thought was called Alice or Stacy and a younger one, whose name he didn't know. They had sat together in the coach on each of the journeys these past three days, chattering.

"Ladies," said Solomon, "are you okay?" Neither responded.

"Alice?" said Nakata, gently. Still, neither moved. "Stacy?" This elicited a flicker, a turning of the head. The older woman peered at them, blinking; Nakata saw the focus return to her eyes.

"Are you hurt? Did you scream?" asked Solomon.

"Scream? No. Did someone scream?" she replied. As if in response, another guttural yelp sounded, choking down into a wet moan.

"Go back to the van. Mr Tidyman will look after you," said Solomon. Stacy rose, taking the other woman's arm and guiding her to her feet.

"I don't know what happened," she said. "We were looking around, and then we were. . ." She broke off, unsure and then finished, "We sat down for a rest."

Nakata wanted to ask them, *Why?* Why rest in the middle of walking around a strange house? What did you see? Hear? How did it feel? He didn't speak, though, knowing Solomon was right, that to speak would destroy any claim to independence and validity that the experiment might have. Instead, he started to follow Solomon and the women back down the hallway to the stairs, noticing before he left the kitchen that both women had left their notebooks on the table. He picked them up and tucked them into his jacket pocket.

A clatter of voices came from upstairs, three or four overlapping. Heads of light played across the ceiling at the top of the stairs, the beams making the dust in the air glitter briefly. Solomon ran up the stairs, his own torch beam joining the others, a crisscrossing lattice like searchlights in a distant sky, his body creating a black absence against the lights. Nakata followed, keeping close. There was a moment when he was right behind Solomon, when he could smell the man's aftershave, something old and spiced, and he almost bumped into him but held himself back, afraid. He was struck by another sudden image, of catching Solomon's shadow and disappearing into it, becoming lost, only to emerge again from the front door, bleeding out of its pitch mouth in slices every time it was opened.

The stairs opened into a narrow hallway filled with people. They were knotted around a doorway, one of them of them at its centre rattling the door. "It's stuck," said a voice. Another, louder, said, "It's locked from the inside."

"Ladies, gentlemen," said Solomon, stepping easily into the melee. He was a small man, slight and shorter than Nakata, but he seemed to easily take charge, become a centre of calming attention. Torchlight danced across him and he raised a hand to stop it blinding him, saying, "Please point the torches at the walls or floor, if you can." Immediately, the lights steadied, stabilising, drawing the rhythm from the jittering shades.

"He's been screaming," said a third voice. "Inside. He's locked the door."

"Who is it?"

"Mike, we think," said the second voice. Nakata thought it was the jury's foreman, Connelly or Kenelly, something like that. "I was in the hallway when he screamed the first time, then the door slammed shut and he screamed again. He'd been walking around with me, and we'd done most of the other rooms; this was the last one."

"The back bedroom," said Solomon. He didn't sound as professional just then, the smooth exterior brittling for a second before reforming. "That's fine, everyone, we'll take it from here. Please, all go to the van. Mr Tidyman's waiting for you there and has refreshments, I believe."

A babble of voices rose but was quelled by Solomon speaking loudly, "Please, please, this is nothing to worry about."

As the jurors went past, Nakata took one of their torches, wanting to feel less in Solomon's shadow both figuratively and literally. As they descended the stairs, the hallway grew darker, the gloom gathering around them. Solomon tried the door handle, which turned easily. The door did not open. "This is where it happened," he said, almost conversationally. "There's no lock on the door. None of the doors in Stack's Farm have locks except the front and rear external doors. If there's no lock, why won't this open?"

"He might have fallen against it inside," said Nakata, and saw Solomon latch onto his explanation thankfully.

"Yes!" he said. "That must be it! He's fainted or had a fit, and now he's blocking the doorway."

Nakata leaned against the door, turning the handle and pushing. The door didn't move at all. "Hello," he called, pressing his ear to the door. The room beyond was silent.

Silent? No. There was a noise, low and rumbling, and under it the sound of someone crying. Whoever it was, Mike presumably, was sobbing uncontrollably, raggedly. "We need to open this door," Nakata said to Solomon. "He's inside, but I don't think he's in front of the door. He sounds awake." Solomon didn't reply.

Turning back to the door, Nakata called, "Mike, can you hear me? Mike, I need you to concentrate on me, concentrate on my voice. What's blocking the door, Mike, can you see? Try and open the door, Mike. It'll be fine." *I hope*, he thought, *I hope it'll be fine. I have faith, faith and hope, and not much else.* "Mike, can you hear me?"

Nakata tried to open the door again, and this time it gave an inch and then slammed back against him, jolting him away from the woodwork and making him stumble. "Solomon, help me!" he shouted, jumping back and pushing against the door again. It shifted, yawning open several inches, wavering, collapsing back. "Solomon, for God's sake!" he called, looking over his shoulder.

Solomon was standing in the centre of the hallway, looking along it from the stairs to the far end. His face was slack, his mouth open and his eyes wide. Nakata looked along the hall; at its far end was a window through which the night sky peered. The shadows around the window were shifting, thickening, forming into a spindle shape that stretch up either side of the window and joined over its upper edge. The shape moved forward, coming together into a single tall figure, its upper edge brushing against the ceiling with a rasping noise, its skinny arms outstretched and dragging against the wall. Rags hung from it, looping down in swinging strands. Twin pinpricks of redness glowered at them from in its what? Face? Nakata didn't know. The thing took another step towards them, and Solomon moaned, throwing himself against the door.

Under the combined weight, the door gave another few inches, a strip of darkness showing between the door and the jamb. Mike's crying fell from it, disjointed, hoarse. "Push!" Solomon cried, and they pushed. Nakata's feet slithered back across the carpet, the edges of his boots catching in the thick nap. The door opened another couple of inches, and Nakata had the strangest impression that they were being *allowed* to open it, not because they were stronger than whatever was holding it, but because it was amused by their efforts. He threw a look over his shoulder at the shape down the hallway.

It was moving.

It took a step forward, arms dragging the walls, head bobbing down, and then fell across the window and onto all fours. *Two legs, four legs*, Nakata thought randomly: *are they legs at all?* It scuttled along the hall, wavering, uneven, crashing against first one wall and then the other, moving slowly but speeding up. Where the starlight played across it pockmarked flesh showed, craterous and dank, and as it came it made a whining sound, air expelling from lungs and along a throat that was torn and loose. Solomon moaned again, and they pushed. The door bucked forward another two inches and stopped. From inside the room, Mike cried out again, the sob escalating to a scream. The kettle-whistle screech of the thing moving along the corridor increased in volume and intensity, the scrape of its feet (claws? hands? hooves?) along the floor setting Nakata's teeth on edge, dragging gooseflesh up across his skin. He thrust his shoulder against the door again, trying to hit it at the same time as Solomon. There was a dull crack as the wood around the handle splintered, and it swung further open.

Solomon fell to his hands and knees, half in the doorway and half in the hall. Nakata, carried forward by his momentum, tripped over him and staggered headlong into the room. The door, moving freely now, swung wide; the room capered with three torch beams, Nakata's and Solomon's falling in from the doorway and the third elongated across the floor from the dropped torch of the man in the corner.

Nakata hit the floor hard. It was varnished wood, not carpeted, and the impact jolted up his arms and snapped his head back so that his teeth clicked together fiercely. He rolled over, still scrambling crablike away from the door, in time to see the corridor thing appear in the doorway behind Solomon. Before he could call out, it had raised itself behind the other man. Nakata had the impression of old leather and a belly rotted down to blackness, a head swinging back and forth, lips shrivelled back from yellowed teeth. It took a wavering step towards Solomon and then collapsed. Like the tall figure they had seen by the cars, it seemed to dissipate as it fell, strands of it tearing away into the darkness, dissolving in the spastic torchlight until nothing was left of it but dust and memories. Solomon moaned again, his head bowed, looking at Nakata through the dropping curls of lank hair across his forehead. "What was it?" he said.

"A demon," said the man in the corner, unexpectedly. Both Nakata and Solomon looked over at him; he was still pulled into a tight ball, shrinking back into the place where the walls met, but his head was raised. There was dust on his face, streaked with reddened tear tracks. "It came out of the wall. It made a noise like an animal, and the door shut, and suddenly I felt so frightened, so fucking scared and sad."

"Yes," said Nakata, thinking of Wisher, of Lake and Wardle, of faith and the things that made people believe: sight, sometimes; smell, hearing, and often touch. *Proof*, normally, but also just knowing, just having faith in faith itself. Whatever had lurched down the hallway after them, whatever had been in this room, it was gone now; he could feel the difference in the house, like a static charge had been earthed, had flowed away to nothing. Nakata had his own faiths, he was coming to realise, had his own ways of reading places and feeling them. *Perhaps it's like malaria*, he thought, *an initial infection followed by recurring bouts of it.* Already, he could feel the power, whatever it was, filling the room, swirling and eddying in its corners, thickening the shadows and making the torchlight dry and friable.

"You're safe now, though, Mike. Stand up. You, too, Solomon. It's safe, but we have to go. Now."

It took them several minutes to get Mike to his feet; initially, he resisted them, and even after he calmed down, he seemed exhausted, unable to bear his own weight. They had to help him, one either side, supporting him, before they could get him moving, and even then their progress was slow. All the while Nakata could feel the power building, the charge growing, sloshing around the edges of the room in increasingly heavy waves. It pressed against him, bitter and strong, accumulating to the point where it could spark free. And then what? Another demon emerging in the room, slamming the door shut, trapping them? Another spindle thing in the hallway? Something new? He had no desire to find out.

They made it as far as the stairs before it reached its tipping point; Nakata felt it flash to something that wasn't life behind them. He pushed Solomon and Mike ahead of him, glancing back over his shoulder. The shape was already forming around the window, accreting out of the dust and shadows, fleshless limbs emerging, glittering red dots that might have been eyes blinking open. "Move," he said, "and don't stop."

As they descended, Nakata heard the sound of the hallway thing again, the sound of it scraping along the corridor, slurred but sharpening, increasing in speed. He knew, without knowing how, that it had passed the doorways lining the corridor and was coming after them. "Move," he said again, pushing against Mike's back, pushing him forward, "move *now!*"

Mike stumbled at the bottom, staggering, crying out. He fell against Solomon, and the two went to the floor in a struggling pile. Nakata hauled Mike up, pulling him to his feet, pushing him towards the doorway, saying, "Go," dragging at Solomon. The air in the stairwell above them congealed into a moving shape, hunched and thin, clattering down towards them faster and faster. Solomon stumbled again and Nakata dragged him prone, not waiting for him to make it to his feet. Mike hit the door; Nakata expected it to resist him, but it did not, opening easily and then Mike was through and Nakata was behind, Solomon's jacket collar clenched in his fist. The thing behind them wailed, low and hoarse and escalating and then they were through the door as well, staggering into the night's embrace and free.

"Are you okay?" asked Tidyman, standing besides the van, but Nakata didn't answer. Nothing emerged from the doorway behind them, nothing moved in the farmyard besides Tidyman and them.

"How many are on the coach?" asked Solomon, finding his breath in amongst the gasping.

"Nine," said Tidyman, looking more puzzled. "Ten with this gentleman here." Nakata looked back at the house; no torch beams flickered in its windows, and it had already taken on the appearance of an abandoned place.

"Where are the other two?"

"The cowshed," said Nakata. "There are two in the cowshed."

There was something hard in Nakata's pocket. He took it out, finding that *it* was actually *them*, Stacy and the other juror's notebooks from the kitchen table. He opened the top one, reading, *Lounge – cold.* A little further on he found another sentence, *Kitchen – much colder, breath misting.* His researchers had installed thermometers in each room, they could check whether the temperature was actually different or not; it might be a useful correlation, or it might not. Wearily, he climbed onto the coach. The jurors, ten of them, looked at him expectantly and for a moment their pale faces looked like ghosts, ghosts or children, awaiting direction. Nakata had nothing to give them, nothing except selfish practicalities. He went to the women from the kitchen, held out their books to them. "We'll be leaving soon," he said to the occupants of the van at large. "Everyone please make as detailed a set of notes about the farm as you can. Please don't talk to each other until you've finished." Leaving them, he exited the van and started toward the cowshed.

After a moment, Solomon joined him. In the bright light from the lamps, his face was a washed-out pink, flushed across his cheeks but almost white around his eyes.

"What happened here?" asked Nakata.

"I was going to ask you the same question," said Solomon. "What was that?"

"I don't know," replied Nakata. "I didn't mean tonight, I meant before."

"I thought you didn't want to know that," said Solomon. His lawyer's smoothness was creeping back already, weaving across and through him like armour plate.

"I don't," said Nakata. "I mean before all of that, before everything that's brought us here."

"Before?" said Solomon. "Well, the murdered man had owned it for two years. He was rich; that was what attracted the young man at the centre of this whole situation, I suspect. Before that, the farm had belonged to the Stack family for generations."

"Why did they sell?" They were almost at the shed door now, and this suddenly seemed important.

"They went out of business. They didn't modernise, couldn't keep up. The foot and mouth outbreak was pretty much the last straw. They struggled on for a year or so, but then the bank called in the debts. They couldn't pay, so that was it."

"That was it?"

Solomon was quiet. "No," he said after a moment. "Not quite. Old man Stack pulled what was left of his cattle into the cowshed and slaughtered them."

Nakata didn't speak. Slaughtered cattle, a human driven to inhumane acts by desperation and futility and anger. "And?" There was more, he could hear the unspoken sentences gathering in Solomon's mouth. They were at the shed door.

"Then he went into the house, covered in the cows' blood, and killed himself."

"Where?" but knowing the answer without really needing to ask the question.

"He hung himself. In the back bedroom," said Solomon, "where we found Mike."

Nakata felt nothing, no surprise, no dawning realisation. He knew, had known from the moment the thing appeared in the hallway. He had one more question.

"And there's nothing here now? The farm isn't a going concern?"

"No."

Nakata nodded. The barn wasn't empty; he could hear cows.

The barn had a large roller door, but in its centre was a half-open smaller door, man-sized. Nakata pulled it all the way open, letting out a rush of air and noise. It smelled of fresh shit and old blood, of grass and hay and soured milk. Without stepping in, he aimed his torch beam into the body of the building; it caught on hanging straps and pipes thick with dust.

"It's the milking shed," said Solomon. His voice wavered, finding words to fill a silence rather than because information was needed. "I remember reading that, that they'd spent a lot of money upgrading the house and buildings and equipment." Nakata thought of the kitchen, with its new fixtures and fittings, and nodded.

"I think he fancied himself a gentleman farmer," continued Solomon. "He'd made money in some kind of dotcom industry and wanted to get back to the earth, or something." They both looked down at the churned, muddy ground beneath their feet, and then looked at each other, a moment of companionship.

"Let's go," said Nakata, and they went into the barn.

The milking equipment was in the centre of the building, arachnid tangles of pipes and nozzles dangling from the ceiling, clusters of fatter pipework leading away to the far side of the building, and around them were cows.

They were dead, each one spattered with blood, throats mangled and heads torn. *An axe*, thought Nakata, *he used an axe.* The creatures were in stalls that were no longer there, pressed against metal strutted dividers that glimmered, half-seen and insubstantial. Nakata could hear them, hear their laboured breathing whistling through throats that were sliced and mangled. The air stank of their blood and fear, of their deaths, and the dark liquid gathered in pools around their feet. Their eyes were wide, their tongues lolling. Ear tags twitched and shifted as the animals watched them. One or two lowed plaintively.

"Ignore them, I don't think they can hurt you," said Nakata, He hoped he was right. "We need to find the jurors and go."

"There," said Solomon. His voice was slack. Nakata glanced at him; he was staring at the dead animals around them with a look on his face that Nakata couldn't quite recognise. Awe, possibly-awe and fear and belief and disbelief mingling, struggling, vying with each other. He raised a shaking hand and pointed to the far end of the barn. At the end of the long metal runs, beyond the railings and machinery, were two human figures. Neither was moving.

Nakata went to them quickly, and Solomon followed. The figures were men, Nakata saw when he got there, and both were covered in blood. One still held his notebook in one hand and his pencil in the other, and Nakata gently removed them, putting them in his pocket. The book had blood on its cover, warm and slippery, and it smeared across his fingers as he took it. "Can you hear me?" he asked. From behind them, the cows were growing restive, moving more, crying out more.

"Your attention, please," said Solomon, all lawyer now, clicking his fingers in front of the men. Nakata could see him battening down his fear, putting aside the knowledge of what was behind them, and was suddenly struck with admiration for the man. He snapped his own fingers, and one of the men blinked hazily, much like Alice or Stacy had done in the kitchen. Struck by a sudden flash of something, Nakata turned quickly. The cows flickered briefly, as though they were fading from focus, before snapping back into existence. *It's us,* he thought wildly. *It's us! We give them their existence, like a motor powering up a neon light, and then they're here! We brought the man back to consciousness, and for a moment they lose his charge, but they're here now and don't need as much to stay. We're like batteries or power packs; we start things off, but we aren't needed once they're going.* Nakata turned back; both jurors were coming to now. One of them looked around, seeing the cows and starting.

"What the fuck!" he said.

"Ignore them," said Solomon. "We're going."

"There's hundreds," said the other man. "How are they fitting? Why are they covered in blood?" He looked down at himself, realised apparently for the first time that he, too, was covered in blood, and shrieked. Nakata looked back at the cows to find that the man was right; there were more of them, more than could fit in the barn, overlapping and moving, coming out from their stalls and blocking the way back to the door. They gathered in a thick wall, pressing forward. They had solidity and weight as they backed the four men up against the wall, jostling them, their smell rich around them, their sides slick with fluids, bumping and banging and pushing. The pressure grew; the creatures closed in, squeezing, snorting, their breath warm and fetid and cold all at once, heads swaying, jerking, axe-marked flesh opening and clos-ing, wounded mouths gaping and glistening. It was getting hard to breathe, hard to move. Solomon looked at Nakata, pleading. *He thinks I know what to do, but I don't*, he thought. *I never did. Tidyman thought I knew, as well, but they're both wrong, all wrong. I just believed, not in me or Amy or the future or the past, but in the existence of something else. I had faith, and look where it's brought me.* The cows shifted, pressed, advanced. Nakata managed another tightening breath, managed to loose one arm and reached out for Solomon. Solomon took Nakata's outstretched hand and nodded, wheezing. One of the jurors spoke, a muttered female name. A wife? A child? Nakata didn't know, didn't care. He was dying here, dying in a barn. *Amy*, he thought, *Amy, I'm coming. Be there for me, I love you, I miss you.*

"What's going on?" said a voice. Nakata managed to twist, his vision darkening, the edges bleeding in and tunnelling to a point. It was Tidyman, standing in the barn's doorway, tiny yet solid. He walked into the barn, shining a torch about. Where his beam landed on the cows, they faded, where his flesh touched them they melted, pouring down and away, trickling out in long strings to join the blood on the floor, lightening to the mere normality of darkness. Tidyman strode, as inexorable as an icebreaker, that puzzled look on his face, and the cows parted around him. Where he touched them, where they came into contact with his pressing belly and flapping coat, they sizzled and spat, vanishing with a noise like meat sitting on heated metal.

"What are you four doing, huddled together like that?" he asked as he reached them. "Hugging?" He was laughing, grinning.

"Something like that," said Solomon through ragged breaths. Nakata inhaled deep, air that still stank of excrement and mud and long-ago death, air that had never tasted so sweet. The bloodstains across their clothing were fading away, the warm wash of it evaporating. Nakata watched as the dark patches across Solomon's coat bled back to nothing and the patches smearing all of them dwindled until they were gone.

They were clean.

"Let's go," said Tidyman, and they walked back to the van through a barn that was empty and silent.

Nakata 8: Public Gallery, Courtroom 2

"What happened there?"

Nakata was waiting, as was everyone; the jury was expected back any minute now. All of the evidence, his own included, had been given; all of the arguments made. The young man, the accused, was waiting with the rest of them, his dark head lowered to the desk in front of him. Tidyman and his team sat around him; Solomon and his team sat across the courtroom. Curtin was in his judge's chair, watching, impassive.

"What happened there?" It had been the last question Solomon had asked Nakata in cross-examination, a question Nakata thought wasn't so much to do with what he had spoken about in court as it was to do with what he'd *not* spoken about. They had agreed, him and Solomon, that they would not mention what they had experienced, for fear of muddying the water in some way. Let the jury decide, they had agreed. Let the court use the evidence of the experiment, of the recorded testimony of the jurors, of the young man himself, but not of Nakata and Solomon themselves. Besides, what could he say, besides *I don't know?* That they had seen and felt and heard ghosts? That his own faith had been vindicated? That they had been saved by a man who professed no faith, had no apparent way of perceiving what they had both seen? In the end, all he could say was, "We don't know what happened, but something did." *I have tried to show that there are places we can't yet understand, that there are places where the quietness lets some of us experience things differently, but it doesn't mean anything, only our own experiences give us understanding. There's no sense to it,* Nakata thought, *only the commitment we make to what we want the world to be.*

The jury was filing in now. "Don't believe any of the clichés," Tidyman had said. "They might look at him, or me, or the judge, whether they've found him guilty or not, innocent or not. They might look for you, or their relatives in the gallery. They might look down." Most were looking down. The foreman passed a slip of paper to the clerk of the court, who passed it up to Curtin.

"Have you reached a verdict?" asked Curtin.

"Yes, your honour," said the foreman.

"Please tell us what it is," said Curtin.

The courtroom waited.

Acknowledgements

It's my name on the cover, and I'm responsible for the contents, but this book could not exist without the support, love, guidance, advice and occasional nag from the following people:

My family, without whom there'd be no me. Blame them, ladies and gentlemen—it's probably their fault;

All at Dark Continents, who took a chance when I said, *Hey, I've got this great idea for a book...* and then believed me when I told them I could write it;

Steve Marsh, who is still a Krautrock aficionado, a barrister, the father of my godchild and my best mate. I don't see him often enough;

Huw Lines, a Welsh transplant in Taiwan and all-round dude. First drink's still on me, fellah;

Andrew Worgan, for the whiskey and the friendship and the website and the Family Mahone CD;

The Monkeyrack Mob - Mollie Baxter, Norman Hadley, Ron Baker and Sarah Fiske, the nicest, most talented and friendliest bunch of poets, actors and authors I've ever spent time in a pub with;

The Critical Circle – Barry Thorley, Chris Thompson, Paul Buschini, Will Mansell, Mark West and everyone else who passes comment on whatever nonsense I send them without either laughing or telling me to get lost. Your time and efforts are appreciated!

Steve Duffy for the friendship and the penis drawings, which have increased the value of my books immeasurably;

Stephen Volk for the coffee and pastries, and for making London a more bearable place when I'm there;

Gary McMahon for the best advice on writing I've ever had: extend your hands, wiggle your fingers and then start typing;

Lawrence C. Connolly, just for being one of the nicest people it's ever been my pleasure to meet;

John L. Probert, whose gleeful collections *The Catacombs of Fear* and *The Faculty of Terror* were an early influence on the development of Quiet Houses;

In no particular order: Stephen Jones, Simon Marshall-Jones, Joel Lane, Barbara Roden , Allyson Bird, Ray Russell, Chris Roden, Gary Fry, Pete Crowther, Johnny Mains, Simon Strantzas, Paul Finch, Sarah Pinborough, Mark Morris and all the other authors, editors and friends who've made me feel welcome, encouraged me and told me when I was being an idiot – cheers!

To everyone else: I'll try to remember you in the next book. For now, know that I appreciate everything you do, whatever it is and whoever you are.

Afterword: Geographies

Quiet Houses was an experiment. I wanted to see if I could write a set of intertwined stories and create a written portmanteau, the kind of thing done so well in the Amicus movies I'd watched and loved as a child, by George Romero and Stephen King in *Creepshow* and by John Probert in his story collections *The Catacombs of Fear* and *The Faculty of Terror* (both highly recommended, incidentally). It was also an experiment to see if I could write stories sited as firmly as possible in the places I go to regularly, that are important to me or have had an impact on my life. My original plan was to only use real venues for each of the stories contained here, and although I didn't quite manage that, there are enough actual places in here for me to be happy.

The Elms, Morecambe

The Elms existed, as did the café that Nakata and Wisher meet in, and I've described them as accurately as I can remember them. The Elms was a wonderful hotel that did great Sunday lunches, and it's where my wife and I held our wedding breakfast and evening celebration over ten years ago. A year after we got married, we went back for our first anniversary meal and we were pretty much the only customers in a dining room that could easily hold 150 people, being served by a waitress who had an idiosyncratic approach to service and who looked to be slightly older than God, and we laughed for most of the evening. The head waiter was an
Old World sort, whose eastern European accent added a touch of courtly mystique to the place. He could do the trick with the champagne, getting it to bubble over the rim of the glass without spilling, a skill I've never mastered. The Elms closed a couple of years ago and is being turned into flats as I write this, and I can't help but think that it's a shame it's ended this way.

The café is based on a café about a mile from The Elms, on Morecambe's seafront, called The Crescent, which served the best cooked breakfast I've ever had. My overriding memory of the Crescent, besides the food, is that the insides of the windows always seemed to be thick with condensation and the walls were stained with years of cigarette smoke. It closed about 4 years ago, and it's now a Costa Coffee. So, I suppose, it goes.

The female ghost in 'The Elms, Morecambe' is real, by the way, but haunts a different hotel. I was told about her by the grandmother of one of my son's friends, and I thought it was such a sad story that I decided to steal it and use it here. I hope she doesn't mind.

The Merry House, Scale Hall

I live in Scale Hall, and all of the history and geography set out in the story are genuine and as accurate as I can make them. The only liberty I've taken with reality is that the road containing the Merry House is actually slightly over Scale Hall's border and into the next parish, Bare.

A version of this story first appeared in the Gray Friar Press anthology *Where the Heart Is*, and was (along with 'The Pennine Tower Restaurant' from my first collection, *Lost Places*) the story in which I first experimented with using detailed true geography and history, finding in the process that I enjoyed it enormously. Without having had the opportunity to produce this story for *Where the Heart Is* and learning what fun it can be to curse and haunt the places I live in and see every day, *Quiet Houses* would probably have turned out to be very different.

Beyond St Patrick's Chapel, Heysham Head

The walk between Half Moon Bay and Heysham village along Heysham Head is one that I do with my wife and child and dogs fairly often, in all kinds of weather, and it's one of my favourites. It's peaceful, the views over Morecambe Bay are excellent and the sound of the sea is wonderfully calming. The ruined church (one of the earliest centres of Christian worship discovered in the UK) and Viking graves are exactly as described in the story, as is Heysham village. Heysham's a lovely place and one day I hope to live there, to be nearer the sea.

I should probably point out that the scariest thing I've ever seen on any of these walks is a dog the size of a small pony with teeth the size and shape of fat guitar picks, and that I have never been chased by disembodied footprints. Maybe someone has, but if so, they've not told me about it.

The Ocean Grand, North West Coast

Based on the Midland Hotel in Morecambe. The Midland has a long and che-quered history, and when I first went there ten years ago it was just before it closed amid accusations of mismanagement and ownership wrangles. Back then, it was a perfect example of faded seaside glamour; it had the most beautiful fixtures and fittings, but they were falling to pieces. We used to go on Saturday evenings and have an after-dinner drink, sitting in a long glass corridor that extended across the rear of the hotel and gave out on magnifi-cent views of Morecambe Bay and, in the distance, the Barrow headlands. It was always freezing in the sun corridor because the heating was never on and half the windows were broken, but it was worth it for the sight of the ocean and the sense of being somewhere that had a foot placed firmly within a magnificent past.

The story came about because I'd read Barry Guise and Pam Brook's ex-cellent history of the Midland, *The Midland Hotel: Morecambe's White Hope* (Palatine Books, 2007) and it made me think about how buildings made to be full of people might feel if they were closed and empty, and about art created to be viewed being alone and going slowly, claustrophobically mad. Gravette and Priest and the art they created for the *Ocean Grand* are very, *very* loosely based on the work and philosophies of the architect Oliver Hill and the artists Eric Gill and Marion Dorn, who designed and decorated the Midland origi-nally, but mostly they're my creations. Make of that what you will.

The Midland, after years of closure, has been completely refitted and has reopened, and looks spectacular. I'd urge you to visit and to have a drink in the new sun corridor or a meal in one of the restaurants. Me, I'm still a little nostalgic for those Saturday nights in the old sun corridor, when we had to keep our coats on because of the cold and when the wind danced in through the broken windows smelling of brine and sand.

Under Great Moore Street, Manchester

I have a number of favourite pubs in Manchester (where I used to live); The *Salisbury*, where I spent most Thursday nights between the ages of 16 and 18, before going on to the sadly missed nightclub, *The Banshee*, and *Copperface Jack's*, where I first realised how attractive my work colleague Wendy was (oh those legs!) and wondered about trying to chat her up (I did, eventually, and have been married to her for almost 11 years, just in case you're wonder-ing). Then there's *The Temple of Convenience. The Temple of Convenience* is housed in a converted underground Victorian lavatory off Oxford Road, and it's tiny and murky and great fun. I don't get to drink there very often, but when I do, I like the sheer perversity of drinking somewhere that used to actually be a toilet, rather than in a pub that merely looks or smells like a toilet. When I came to write this story, I stole a little of *The Temple's* history because it felt like a good history to steal. I have no idea if the Victorians actually named their lavatories or not, but the detail about the bees sometimes being glazed into urinal bowls is absolutely true. I know, I've pissed against them on occasion.

24 Glasshouse, Glasshouse Estate

This isn't based on any one place so much as it is the number of half-finished estates that are currently awaiting the builders' return. The financial collapse of the past couple of years has meant that they've become a common sight, the buildings boarded and half-formed, abandoned by firms that cannot afford to finish the building and cannot sell what they haven't completed. There's something slightly creepy and maudlin about these deserted places where life hasn't even begun to flower, places without even ghosts to keep them company. Sometimes, work on these little clusters of buildings resumes; often, it doesn't.

The Glasshouse Estate is named for the offices the charity I work for used to be based in, a great rambling building in a London street called Glasshouse Yard, a name I always thought needed to be used in a ghost story. Wardle is named after the boss of a friend of mine who treated his workers appallingly (so I'm told) and who will, if there's any justice, feel the weight of the karmic wheel bearing down on him soon.

Stack's Farm, Trough of Bowland

Based, very loosely, on the farm an ex-girlfriend's parents lived in, a weird mix of older stone buildings and new barns with tubular steel frames and sheet walls. Although I didn't spend much time there, the visits I did make were always interesting, but not in ways that I'd hoped or expected. I had the dubious pleasure of being given the opportunity to help artificially inseminate the pigs during one stay there, and to drink milk still warm from the cow on another. On a third, I was asked to help chase an escaped cow and watched as it got up a head of steam and then jumped over a four-foot-high hedge, mooing furiously. Two of these opportunities I enthusiastically took to, one I turned down; I'll leave you to guess which was which.

These stories have been fun to write. I've enjoyed searching out places, populating them with ghosts and demons, giving the characters in my head voices and faces and lives, and then occasionally taking those lives away again. It's fashionable, at the moment, for people to talk a lot about journeys, the *journey* they're on, or a character's on, or a reality TV show contestant's *journey* and the trials they've faced, but the journey's not the real point, not always. Journeys are about the leavings and arrivings of life, they lead to *places*, mostly noisy, occasionally quiet, hopefully fascinating and vital and welcoming, sometimes cold and dark and dangerous. This collection is about the places at the end of the journey.

I like Nakata; he'll be back.

Simon Kurt Unsworth
July 2011

Simon Kurt Unsworth was born in Manchester in 1972 on a night when, despite extensive research, he can find no evidence of mysterious signs or portents. He currently lives on a hill in the north of England with his wife and child awaiting the coming flood, where he writes essentially grumpy fiction (for which pursuit he was nominated for a 2008 World Fantasy Award for Best Short Story). He is tall, grouchier than he should be and the owner of a selection of really rather garish shirts. His work has been published in a number of critically acclaimed anthologies, including the critically acclaimed *At Ease with the Dead, Shades of Darkness, Exotic Gothic 3, Gaslight Grotesque, Never Again* and *Lovecraft Unbound*. He has also appeared in three of Stephen Jones' *Mammoth Book of Best New Horror* anthologies (19, 21 and 22), and also *The Very Best of Best New Horror*. His first collection of short stories, *Lost Places*, was released by the Ash Tree Press in 2010, and he has a further collection, *Strange Gateways*, due out from PS Publishing in 2012. His as-yet-unnamed collection will launch the Spectral Press *Spectral Signature Editions* imprint in 2013, so at some point he needs to write those stories. You can follow him on Facebook or Twitter and he might eventually get his website up and running, but don't hold your breath.

A New Breed of Publishing

visit us @

www.darkcontinents.com

Lightning Source UK Ltd.
Milton Keynes UK
UKOW050310180911

178852UK00001B/36/P